an accident waiting to happen

About the author

Adrian White is an English writer who has lived with his family in Ireland for over twenty-five years. *An Accident Waiting to Happen* was first published by Penguin Books in 2004. His second novel, *Where the Rain Gets In*, was also published by Penguin in 2006. His third novel, *Dancing to the End of Love*, is published by Black & White Publishing.

an accident waiting to happen

ADRIAN WHITE

Lynskey Books

This edition published 2016 by
Lynskey Books
Originally published by Penguin Books, 2004
All rights © 2016 Adrian White

Paperback ISBN: 978-1-911013-32-7

Typesetting by Dinky Design
Printed in the EU

Praise for *An Accident Waiting to Happen*

Adrian White's debut is irresistible ... it's like life.
AFRIC HAMILTON, IRISH EXAMINER

If you were to judge a book by its cover, you might think An Accident Waiting to Happen is a touchy-feely boy's book in the Tony Parsons/ Nick Hornby tradition. However, appearances can be deceptive and this is a rather unpleasant book with a remarkably unsympathetic narrator. Dark, unsettling – and definitely not touchy-feely.
ANNA CAREY, IMAGE

A tough subject, desertion, handled with compelling simplicity as a father and son cope alone in a rough world. Extraordinarily engaging and sensitive, wringing one's emotions.
SARAH BROADHURST, THE BOOKSELLER

His novel mixes gripping sections with an internal monologue filled with anxiety, confusion and weakness. Disturbing and sometimes irresistible, this is a story that will find a responsive audience in the growing ranks of dispossessed fathers.
LUCILLE REDMOND, IRISH INDEPENDENT

White offers a porthole on the male dilemma – the pressure to plumb his emotions and articulate them, the quandary of a sense of alienation from his environment. His unflinching honesty, coupled with an accessible writing style, produce an assured debut.
MARTINA DEVLIN, EVENING HERALD

Praise for *Where the Rain Gets In*

He has fashioned both an engaging casino-sting/ caper story and a wiser, psychologically detailed tale of hard-won success, unrequited love and hidden personal pain.
HUGH TYNAN, IRISH EXAMINER

White has described his characters brilliantly and, in a feat that is not easy for any male author, has drawn a picture of an incredibly believable female character. Although White's characters appear to be damaged and hurt beyond repair, this book leaves the reader with a sense that there is hope. Very well written and with such a fantastic title, how could you resist?
BIBLIOFEMME

It's a challenging book about a woman who cuts herself. It helps you get inside the character's head and understand self-loathing. It's exceptionally well written.
MARTINA DEVLIN, IRISH DAILY STAR

One

My friends tell me that if I'm so keen to be a writer then I should get out more and go see the world. What good does it do me to sit at home with a typewriter all day? Surely I'd learn more about life if I actually set about living it a little?

Well, I say to them, if I lived the lives I see others live there'd be no time left to write about it. This is disappointing for my friends – both of them – who obviously believe that as a writer I should be living life to the full. (What do they want – for me to take off to Nicaragua? Pick coffee? Would that help defeat the Contras? Or make me a better writer?) I see so much from this chair that I'd be crazy to go looking for more. It's scary out there. I can't even make up my mind if I should be buying or boycotting South African oranges – which is the more likely to end apartheid? I have enough going on in my own world, thanks; at least this way I manage to maintain some form of control.

Already I see enough, often I see too much. I certainly hear too much. I hear John and Sarah upstairs kicking the shit out of each other – but mainly John kicking the shit out of Sarah. I hear Sarah scream, stop, you're hurting me, and I hear John continue to slap her about. Punch her, I mean. What do I do? Nothing – I don't know what to do. You see, even in my own tiny little world, I never know what's best. Am I supposed to leave them be – like almost every other time – or is this going to be the time when it goes too far? Would I be thanked for interfering or would even Sarah tell me to mind my own business?

Though it is my business: I can't sleep for their fighting and Caitlin is physically sick at the violence. I lie in bed while she throws up in the bathroom.

"Make them stop," she shouts but I don't know how. I know how strong John is; maybe I don't know it as well as Sarah does right now, but I know he's a big guy. If it came to a standoff then I wouldn't have a chance. Though John is about my height, and not particularly well built, you can see at a glance that his job as a stonemason has made his body as hard as the material he works on. Our son Tomas once had us all laughing by trying to lift John's bag of tools off the ground; I'm not sure I could lift it any easier yet the weight barely registers with John as he flings the bag across his back.

Should I call the cops? Could I bring myself to call the cops and if I did, would they have the power to do anything? John and Sarah are married now and this puts Sarah outside the protection of the law – so long as John hits her quietly. Carry on, but don't create a disturbance. Maybe John should gag Sarah and then we wouldn't hear her scream? Caitlin called the cops on them once and that made John think twice – but only twice – and normal service soon resumed. He was trying to kick in the front door because Sarah had locked him out and we had to listen at first to the pleading, and then the threats, and then the assault against the door. Caitlin and I lay there in the darkness, hoping and praying that this would be the time when John was finally gone for good, but Sarah gave in and opened the door. The cops arrived over an hour later and their lecture to John and Sarah was all about noise and disturbing the neighbours, as though this was the point. They weren't around later to hear the dull thumps: Sarah paying the price for locking John out.

It was Caitlin who first told me what a husband could do to his wife, if not with the full blessing of the law then at least with the law powerless to stop it. I know things are changing, now we're in the middle of the enlightened Eighties, but there's still some way to go. When Caitlin told me what Imran did to her, I couldn't walk through the streets of Rusholme without hating every Paki in sight. I blamed them all for what he'd done to Caitlin. Of course, hating Pakis didn't get me anywhere and now I have John upstairs to show how it takes all sorts.

So, you see what I mean about never knowing what to do? Caitlin does – she comes through from the bathroom, bangs on the ceiling with the heel of a shoe and shouts for them please to stop. She's living through each and every sound they make. Her shouting seems to have an effect. Perhaps the realisation that we can hear every smack gives John pause before hitting her again – some feeling of guilt perhaps, though I doubt it. Either way, he stops and we can try to get back to sleep. Caitlin is returning to work tomorrow after being off sick for a week.

Sarah tries to make light of it when I see her in the morning.

"Aren't you going to ask me why I'm wearing sunglasses?" Her kids cling on to her legs as she hangs out her washing. The things we have to put up with as neighbours, eh?

Yeah, yeah, I think, until he hits you again tonight. Believe me Sarah, I don't need to ask; I hear everything from this typing chair, I hear it all. I just don't know what to do about it.

When Caitlin and I return to the clinic at the hospital for what turns out to be the last time, we're surprised to be seen first by a social worker. I guess this is a giveaway but at the time it just seems odd – social workers are a part of other people's lives, not ours. Not that anything much comes of it. Inane questions like 'How do you think you would feel?' don't do much for me.

"It would destroy me," says Caitlin.

I look up and across at her, not understanding why she'd even answer this stranger, let alone tell her how she'd feel. I evade the woman's questions; I haven't figured out yet how I'd feel – haven't even figured out what I'm supposed to be figuring out – so I'm not about to start sharing it with some social worker.

"You weren't so nice to that woman," Caitlin says, once we've been left alone.

"Well, how the fuck should I know how I'd feel?"

"Maybe we're about to find out," says Caitlin.

The doctor's much better than the social worker; this couldn't be easy for her. Turning first to Caitlin's file, she outlines what we already know. This is reassuring and easy to follow.

"When it comes to any possible side effects your infection

may have had," she says to Caitlin, "you'll be glad to hear that this has completely cleared up. There's no damage to the womb and absolutely no reason why you shouldn't have children. The pain you're in at the moment is a different matter but we can sort that out now we know there's nothing else wrong with you."

She turns to my file and uses the same trick, repeating what I know to put me at my ease.

"You had an operation when you were twelve and we thought this might well have affected the fertility of your sperm."

Yes, go on.

"Well, I doubt if the operation itself did any harm but the fact you had it so late probably did. In fact, the results of your semen analysis show that your sperm count is so low as to be virtually negligible. This would explain why Caitlin has not become pregnant."

"Yes, it would," I say.

Fuck! We didn't even come to the doctor for this. This started with Caitlin being in so much pain each month and now we're here being told we're not to have children?

"I'm sorry," says the doctor.

"Yes," I say.

I'm thinking back to being twelve, listening to a doctor telling my parents to wait; telling them it was best to let nature take its course. Well, nature was taking its course all right but not in the way we expected. I mention this to the doctor here at the hospital.

"Yes, that was medical opinion at the time but now we know better. I'm sorry."

Caitlin is crying, I can see Caitlin crying by my side.

"Even if they'd operated earlier," continues the doctor, "the damage would already have been done."

The doctor's a good doctor. She doesn't baulk at telling us the bad news and her manner lets us know she understands just how painful this will be. But she doesn't let us dwell – she points out that unlike some couples we're lucky to have Tomas,

Caitlin's five-year-old son from her marriage to Imran. There are other options open to us; this isn't the end of the story. Take a breather, she's saying, and then let's see how we go on from here. Somehow I get Caitlin out of there and home.

They say accidents can happen but I don't know.

Take Leta for instance. There she is driving along, oblivious to the Greater Manchester Transport bus that's about to send her all the way to Stepping Hill Hospital. She pulls up to the red light and it's as though she's waiting for the accident to happen. It's long past midnight and this usually busy junction is deserted but for Leta's sexy little Mini – and, of course, our late night bus service. Leta turns to Maria, her mother, in the passenger seat but Maria is fast asleep. Leta looks in the rear view mirror to catch her boyfriend's eye and sees instead the fast approaching bus, brmm brmm, pull up to the bumper baby, and then it's happened. The bus just ploughs through them, sending the Mini spinning across the carriageway. As it hits the opposite kerb, the car flips over on to its roof and travels for a further fifty yards along the road, sparks flying, lighting up the dull wet night. The car catches the railings running along the side of the carriageway, flips again on to the wheels, and spins into the path of a car travelling in the opposite direction. Then it's back once again, hard against the railings before finally coming to a stop.

The driver of the second car is experienced and he manages to not over-compensate. The wing of his car is badly damaged but he's OK. He runs back to the mess in the road and watches the rear-lights of the bus disappear into the distance. Leta's mother is lying in the road; she's not going far and she knows it. This kind of thing has happened to her before and right now she's happy to be alive. She understands the nature of accidents; she understands that these things just happen. She can hear Leta screaming but can't lift her head off the pavement to see look at her. She wishes she could tell her daughter, tell Leta, it's useless to scream: this thing has happened, why not let it be?

Leta's boyfriend, Mike, could quite as easily have been the

screamer but Leta's got in there first and this calms him down. Ex-boyfriend, rather – they both know it's over between them so it's doubly unfortunate that this should happen now, tonight of all nights. Earlier in the evening, she had finally admitted that she'd been seeing someone else for months, a guy called Sutcliffe. Mike didn't know which was worse: being told, it being someone with such a wank name, or having to share a lift home with Leta and her mother. And now this?

Mike looks around to see there's no back window, that there's no back anything to the car anymore. Although he started the journey in the back seat, he's now sat next to Leta in the seat left vacant by Maria. In the limited space he has, he turns, grabs hold of Leta's hair, pulls it back and – smack – hits her hard across the face. This shuts her up long enough to see the blood pouring from his ear and then she's off again. Mike knows he's not too badly hurt but he is worried about the smell. Petrol and metal; he remembers the sparks from a lifetime ago and is none too keen on hanging around. Leta's screaming is driving him nuts; she's not even hurt he can't help but notice. How like Leta to be the least hurt and make the most noise. He slaps her again.

Shut the fuck up, can't you?

Mike squeezes through the jagged edges of glass and metal to the cold damp air outside. He finds his feet on the wet tarmac and realises he's lost a shoe. He's not worried about the glass in his feet; they'll sew everything up at the hospital and besides, this isn't really happening to him. He just wants to be away from that car, away from that smell. Who'd have thought the intestines of a car could smell so bad? He reaches in for Leta and, none too gently, pulls her by the arms through the gap. By the time he has her out safely he's had just about enough of her.

Where the fuck is Sutcliffe now? Mike asks, as he dumps Leta on the ground. He doesn't say the words though and he knows he's going to have to go through the motions of caring for her one last time. Is it always like this at the end of something? He crosses over to where Leta's mother is lying in the road. The other driver is stood over her and they agree she can't be moved.

"She's beautiful," says the driver strangely.

"Yes," says Mike and returns to Leta. This is how they are when the ambulance arrives to take them to the hospital. (Meanwhile, the bus driver has gone on to enjoy an orgy of accidents as he makes his way back to the depot. He's angry at being given a night shift at such short notice and pissed out of his mind. When the police finally catch up with him, he really hasn't a clue about the damage he's done.) Back at the hospital, Mike is playing his role to perfection because he knows it's for the last time. The boyfriend – he's even referred to once as the boyfriend. Leta is calmer now and regrets that Mike is involved.

Thanks for looking after me, her look says to Mike, but he's past it. He's here for the night and he'll do what he must but then that's it, he's getting out. Leta knows this and is still grateful. Everyone is so kind (aren't they always?) and when she hears that her mother will be OK she smiles a thank you to the nurse and falls asleep.

It doesn't take long for the results of the tests to damage Caitlin. The immediate effect is as though a car has crashed in her mind. She staggers around, deafened and in a daze. I walk into the kitchen and she's slicing a loaf of bread with a knife, the whole loaf.

"Caitlin? What are you doing?"

She looks down at the knife in her hand, at the slices of bread. For a second I see her grip tighten and then she drops the knife and walks out past me. I begin to pack away the bread but she comes back into the room and sweeps everything on to the floor with her arm.

"You just don't get it, do you?" she screams and walks out again.

I pick up the bread and put it in the bin. I put the knife in the sink for washing but then I remember it's dangerous to leave a knife lying around. I wash and dry the knife and replace it on the rack.

I want to protect Caitlin from what this is doing to her but

I'm the one doing it. From now on everything she thinks, says or does is determined by the fact that we're not going to have children together. She knows immediately how she feels, she knows what it all means and lays herself open to it all. She said, when that social worker first asked, that this would destroy her and now I can see she was right. How can she live in this way? She lives through things as though they're really happening and not just some accident that will pass. For Caitlin, there's no escaping the crash. She doesn't share my accident mentality.

What does she want? Does she want me to scream? Like all the best accidents, there's no way to avoid this and no way to prevent it – so what else is to be done? I don't know what to do so I just keep quiet. I must be driving her crazy. It doesn't seem real at all, like a novel - The Sun Also Rises, maybe - or the movies. I'm glad I don't live through life any more, glad I don't actually have to live through things as they happen. I much prefer it this way.

"Aren't you bitter?" she asks and I don't know who or what to be bitter about. When Camus' Outsider says 'Mother died today', I reckon that that just about covers it; what else is there to say? If something bad happens or something good, then it's immediately obvious whether it's bad or good. I don't know of any better words to use. I'm no use when it comes to the next step, a bit slow, if you like, at grasping any further consequences. I wasn't always this way - I don't know where I heard or when I learned that words are no good. Words are useless and never match up to what I really want to say. I could say things like 'I love you' but I could be lying. It's not that I don't want to say the words and not that I wouldn't mean them if I did; it's just, how can I use words at a time like this? I don't understand what's happening; I don't understand what has been done to me. And at the same time, Caitlin wants to hear the words and when she doesn't, well what is she to believe?

"Do you ever think of Leta?"

Caitlin asks me this as I come through from Tomas's bedroom. I've just finished putting him to bed and I'm looking forward to an early night in preparation for Caitlin returning to work tomorrow. I have a feeling, just a feeling, that maybe things are closing in on normal; that maybe we can beat this thing together, the three of us. It's been a tough week and we have hard times ahead but I believe we can get through it. This is where I'm at – Caitlin is elsewhere. So she asks me the question and I'm clueless as to where it's going. As I said, a little slow.

"I suppose so, yes." I say.

"And what do you think about her?" As I turn to Caitlin I can see she's crying. This has happened so much in the past week that it's difficult to comfort her, however callous that may sound.

"Don't cry." I say.

"You're going back to her, aren't you?"

"To Leta?"

"I read your diary." This doesn't make any sense. I've written no such thing in my diary because I have no diary to write things in. I write shopping lists on scraps of paper and reminders to myself of places to be for Tomas.

"The diary you keep in your drawer," says Caitlin. "I read it today while you collected Tomas from school. I know it was wrong but I did it anyway. I'm sorry."

"But that diary's three or four years old!"

"Then why do you still keep it?"

I don't know the answer to this. I like the idea of knowing where I was and what I was doing over a period of time. I've only kept a diary – a detailed diary – at one time in my life and that was about three years ago, when I first started seeing Leta. I'd known her when she was with Mike but had lost touch when they separated. It was also the time of my first serious attempt to make it as a writer. When I went to throw the diary away recently, I had one last look and chose to keep it. It could have been over any three months; it wasn't what was written that I liked but the owning of a full three months that I'd never forget. I'd like the same for every moment I've been on the planet.

"What did she have that I don't?" asks Caitlin.

Oh Christ, I'm watching the crash as it happens. Caitlin is at the centre of the accident and there's nothing I can do. I can't prevent it from happening. When is an accident not an accident? When you're in it.

I can hold her. I do hold her. But I can't stop her living through it. I could say things like 'Don't be silly' but I could be lying.

"Don't be silly," I say.

Caitlin believes I'm waiting for an opportunity to leave her and Tomas. This isn't rational; this is Caitlin living through the crash. Surely she has more reason to leave me and find someone else while I cling on to Caitlin and Tomas for all they're worth? But Caitlin believes I shall leave her and Tomas and go back to Leta. She believes these things and they are as real to her as if they were already done. Every fear has become a possibility to Caitlin – no, a certainty – and it's killing her. I hold her and I try to reassure her but it will take time for her to feel safe again.

Already the past is bleeding into the present. I don't want Leta back in my life. I want what I have here now.

"I'm going to bed," I say.

Caitlin is being destroyed and all I want to do is to sleep. Things we have had no control over have brought us to this and now all I would like is to sleep. Oh, and for things to be better when I wake.

But of course, it doesn't happen like that – instead we have the John and Sarah show playing upstairs and Caitlin being sick in the bathroom.

Two

Caitlin has always been dangerous and I'm pleased to see some of the edge has returned when we meet for lunch on her first day back at work. Why do I call her dangerous? Because men want her and women are afraid of her. Mary warned me off Caitlin soon after they met, told me I'd be hurt all over again and that she was nothing but trouble. Roger liked Caitlin immediately and Mary hated Roger liking Caitlin immediately. This was the effect Caitlin had on my friends and I've watched it over and over with everyone she meets. Caitlin unnerves people; they're not comfortable with her and she gives them nothing to put them at their ease. Of course, once they get to know her, as Mary has, they either love her or hate her but even then it has more to do with how they feel about themselves than with anything Caitlin might do or say.

Caitlin knows what she believes and she sees things for what they are. She knew how she felt about me as soon as we met and she acted on it. I didn't need too much persuading. I may have blunted some of her sharpness just through the very act of us being together. It didn't take long to find her soft centre. Her short skirts used to be full of provocative contempt, whereas now they're just short skirts. But she has other, more combative qualities and it's good to see them again.

"Just when I wanted an easy time of it," she says. "I wanted to go in to work, clock up my hours and then come home. I wanted nothing more from today." We go across the road to the pub for a drink. As we sit down, Caitlin explains: Charlotte, a new girl, only recently started at the office, had been taken to one side by her section boss and threatened with the sack if her work didn't improve.

"And...?" True to form, I'm a bit slow here.

"He has no powers of hiring or firing. Verbal warning maybe, but there are procedures for that and he didn't follow them." Caitlin says that Charlotte was taken into a room on her own to be intimidated by her boss – and that her boss happens to be a man.

"You should see this Charlotte," she says, "she's gorgeous. And he's alone in a room with her? It's questionable at best; if you think about it long enough then it's sinister. All the more so for going unnoticed by anyone but me."

I shrug. This is the nature of Caitlin's workplace; this is office life for you.

"Who was it?" I ask.

"Harry Horwich."

Ah. Now he would be intimidating, all six feet five of him. It's funny though, my favourite image of Harry Horwich is well away from the workplace. I saw him once being hit on the chin during a soccer match, a dirty, nasty match that kept going off all over the place. This one guy took the opportunity while the ref was distracted to jump up and just stick one on Harry for no reason at all, apart, I guess, from his height. Even though Harry was on my team, it still made me laugh; he was reduced all of a sudden to a hittable size. I thought, if he can be hit here then he can be hit anywhere. I've kept it with me over the years and suggest to Caitlin she tells Charlotte what I know.

"Perhaps then she'll see him as he truly is."

Picture them in the ocean, I always tell myself when I come across the likes of Harry Horwich. There are mountains in the ocean that are larger than Everest and they barely reach the surface.

"Can you have his neck for it?" I ask.

"Doubt it," says Caitlin. "I'm seeing the manager this afternoon but the most he'll do is accept that Horwich was wrong and agree to have a word with him. That's as far as it will go."

I don't know how Caitlin does it. This type of thing goes on day after day and each time she follows it up by bringing it to the manager's attention. And these are her workmates – this is before you throw in the nature of her job, facing the public and assessing their claims for benefits. You'd hope for at least a little support, a hint of team spirit but no, they get fucked from on high by the likes of Harry Horwich. How does Caitlin keep calm when the returns are so low? She says that if she lost her head then she'd lose her job and what good would that do anyone? I see what she means but I still don't know how she does it. For all my talk of mountains and oceans, I know it would be a very different story if I were out there in the world. I don't have Caitlin's patience and tolerance; I wouldn't last two minutes.

I had a little trouble myself recently, in – of all places – the local off-licence. Shopkeepers and I have got along fine since I stopped taking their goods without paying for them. I was a compulsive thief when I was younger – much younger, aged nine or so – and the greater the risk the more compulsive a thief I became. I stole cash, cigarettes, sweets – I can't describe to you the thrill of knowing that if I wanted something, all I had to do was take it. I enjoyed the standard of living and there was the added bonus of cash to spend with my friends and the pleasure and popularity that money can buy. I felt bad about stealing from home but never had a problem with shops; I told myself that no one person was losing out. In fact, it was so easy stealing from shops – I used to shout my thanks as I ran out the store – that the fun didn't last and even the prestige among my friends counted for little in the end.

But that was a long time ago and I certainly wasn't looking for trouble when I went shopping for beer. One can of beer from a four-pack had been flat as I opened it the previous night but the owner of the off-licence thought otherwise.

"You couldn't have had one flat can out of a pack of four," she said. "Maybe all four but not one out the four." She turned to another customer and said, "What they do is have a party and then try to return their half-empty cans."

"The can's full," I pointed out. "If I was on the fiddle then I'd have brought four cans back like you said." I was beginning to wish I'd not bothered, it was only one can after all.

"It's pathetic," she said, again addressing the other customer rather than me. "Here," she said, reaching to the shelf behind her, "if it means so much to you," and she placed a can on the counter. I took it as much from a reflex as anything and walked home. I was astonished. Caitlin was all for me contacting Consumer Affairs or whoever it is but that was no use to me. As I looked at the can on the kitchen table I knew I would never enjoy drinking it, even if I were to leave it and forget about it for a month or so; that beer was always going to leave a bad taste. I waited until I'd calmed down a little and then returned to the shop. The owner was still gossiping and I waited for her attention. She gave me a look, as if to say, 'What now?' and raised her eyebrow to the same customer as before.

"You see what I have to put up with?" she said.

I shook the can in front of her face, opened it and then emptied it over her head. It felt good, it felt really good but I don't think I'll be shopping there again – which is a pain because the next nearest off-licence is miles away.

Later that same evening I still felt happy with what I'd done but I knew I couldn't make a habit of it; sooner or later it would land me in trouble. It was a little like stealing after all – as though I'd gone on a smash and grab raid to the outside world and had better lie low for a while. Caitlin on the other hand is restricted to procedure because she has to work in this outside world. This takes more nerve than any grand gesture of defiance and besides, if she were to resign (which is the grandest gesture she could make in her circumstances) it would suit her employers down to the ground; they would love to see her go.

"I must get back," she says finishing her drink. "Thanks for meeting me."

"What time are you home?" I ask.

"Soon as possible, the earliest I can get away."

As I walk her back to the office, Caitlin apologises for going on about work but I don't mind; anything is preferable to how she was after the hospital. I'd begun to think she was going crazy.

*

For Tomas's first week at school, I was to wait i
building to collect him from the cloakroom. The pu
this was to give him the confidence that I would always
at home time. Before the week was through though,
told me to wait outside with the other parents; he'd s
in the playground. He was fine and didn't want to be tr
in any way different to the other kids. I was pleased for
and relieved for myself. The first day I collected him, I wa
anxious not to be late that I was the first and only parent wai
inside the school. A teacher passed me by and given me a lo
A 'what are you doing there?' look. Didn't ask the question, ju
gave me the look. Before leaving the corridor, she hesitated an
turned and then gave me another one. I obviously didn't loo
like a parent, or her idea of a parent, and my standing there was
suspicious enough to give her cause for alarm. I appreciated
her caution but it's never nice to be mistaken for a pervert. But
then I thought, thank Christ for that! Who the hell wants to
look like a parent anyway?

Now as I arrive at school to meet Tomas I lean against the
outside wall and yawn. I feel like a parent and probably look
like one too. Everyone here needs a good twelve hours sleep,
that's what binds us all together. I know now why I worried
that teacher; I was too wide-awake to be a parent. Each of us
waiting here is programmed to be outside this school at three-
thirty in the afternoon and everything else in our lives amounts
to nothing come home time.

I generally have very little to do with the other parents. I'm
not unpleasant; I just have nothing to say beyond a polite hello
and sometimes a smile. Contrast this with Caitlin who, because
she works, is here nowhere near as often and yet manages to
chat freely with anyone and even appear to know some of the
parents quite well. Maybe I shouldn't be allowed out? I often
construct imaginary lives for some of them as I stand there
waiting. Seeing the same people there each day, mostly their
lives are so transparent it takes little effort to fill in the gaps.
Occasionally though someone will surprise me into correcting

my initial impression. A lot of them seem to know each other, and the ins and outs of their respective lives, and it's obvious their friendships extend to their home lives too. I shy away from such intimacies, not so that I should remain a mystery to them but so that they remain a mystery to me. I much prefer the worlds I create for them than what they'd tell me of their own and besides, I enjoy coming into such close contact with people I know nothing at all about. (Or perhaps I'm incapable of socialising with these other parents and only claim to prefer it this way because I have no choice?)

Sometimes Tomas can stand beside me for a full minute without my realising he's there. At other times he stands blankly by the entrance, as lost in thought as I ever am. Just seeing him makes me smile. I call him over.

"What have you been up to today then?" I ask. He looks down at his shoelace and asks me to tie it for him.

"Nothing much," he says. Going over the same niceties day after day doesn't make much sense to Tomas, although he is sometimes formally polite enough to ask if I've had a good day. It's not until we get close to home that he becomes interested in the world outside school. This is hardly surprising given the change in company from his classmates to me. We also don't live that near to the school so he becomes twice removed from that environment. What Tomas needs is a brother or sister but sorry mate, can't help you there.

A house at the entrance to our estate is blackened by fire.

"When did that happen?" asks Tomas.

"Last night, I guess, otherwise I'd have heard the fire engine this afternoon." There's still smoke coming from the house but it's the damp, dead smoke of a fire long extinguished.

"We didn't see it this morning," says Tomas.

"No, we went out the other way, remember?" Considering the damage done to the interior of the house, it's amazing the fire didn't disturb the whole street. Only the outer shell of the building remains; from where we stand by the kerb we can see nothing but blackness inside. Tomas is finding the scene fascinating so I suggest we walk on. I've no wish to be seen

staring by the tenants should they still be around and, like most people, I want very little to do with somebody else's tragedy.

The road into our estate curves around a corner from the burnt-out house. I prepare myself, as I do each time, for the flat to have been broken into while I was out. It's better this way, and then when everything is OK I can relax, but I'm never going to get caught out again. Every time, on the curve, I take a second, gather my thoughts, toughen myself up and get ready. Great life, eh? Although, if truth be told, we haven't had any bother since we bought a Beta-Max video instead of a VHS; potential thieves can't find a buyer for that old warhorse and besides, no one person could lift it through a window.

Suzie from next door is out doing her garden as we reach home and I ask her if she knows anything about the fire.

"Not a thing," she says, "and you know me, the smallest sound and I'm awake. Mind you, it didn't help having them two at each other's throats again."

John and Sarah; we all live so close it's impossible not to hear.

"You heard them then?"

"Listen," says Suzie, "they enjoy it. They can kill themselves for all I care."

"Who?" asks Tomas. Suzie and I smile. What Suzie's saying is that John and Sarah deserve each other. The only problem is it keeps us awake at night. Sarah knew about John when she married him; we all knew about John when she married him and since then she's gone and changed the tenancy agreement to their joint names. Any hope she had of getting rid of him disappeared when she married him, along with our sympathy. The problem is that Sarah doesn't want to be rid of John; she'd rather this than nothing at all.

"You know she's had her tits done?" says Suzie.

I shake my head and smile.

"Done how?" I ask.

"Made smaller," says Suzie. "Said they were giving her back ache. The rest of the world wants theirs to be bigger and madam has to have hers cut down to size."

"Ugh!" says Tomas but he loves this.

"Suzie…" I say.

"Maybe that's why his lordship's not too happy? Mind you, there was plenty there to go at."

As for the fire, neither Suzie nor I can think who lived at that house and they certainly don't live there any more. I go inside the flat and leave Tomas next door with Suzie while I cook his tea. Tomas is crazy about her. There's also Suzie's daughter Olivia to spoil him and, when he's around, her son Barry for Tomas to worship. Suzie has unlimited time for him and a constant flow of visitors through her open front door. Tomas sits there fascinated; it's much more fun than being home alone with me. It's a deal we have: Suzie minds our child in return for us occasionally minding her stolen goods.

We have a two-bedroom ground floor flat – a living room, a kitchen, the bedrooms and a bathroom. It's just right for us and with the work we've put in it's as much of a home as we need. We're luckier than some in that we have a garden of sorts. The building may belong to the council but as far as we're concerned, the flat is ours. When Caitlin moved in there were no doors or windows, graffiti covered the walls and raw sewage was seeping through the bathroom ceiling from the unoccupied flat upstairs. Loose wiring was strung across from one end of a room to the other, there was no form of heating, and the only place to wash was in a rusty cast-iron bathtub. Sarah moved in upstairs at about the same time; John worked on their flat as I worked on ours.

While I cook Tomas's tea I think of the house fire and what could have happened; it's strange that Suzie would know so little. I think back to the only other house fire I've known and if I'm honest then I'm relieved to have heard nothing last night.

Early one morning – and I mean early, as in dawn in summer when it gets light before it has any business getting light – I heard a woman screaming for help. At first it was still in my dreams and then in that horrible conscious moment when you know something is real, I willed myself to go back to sleep.

"Please, somebody help me, please…"

I told myself it was nothing – a drunk. I checked the time. Shit! It was light already.

"Please!"

If it was a drunk, I could forget her. I hated her already for doing this to me, for including me in her life. What was happening to her, anyway? I thought I knew; I thought she was being raped but I didn't want to be the only person who knew. I was living in the attic room of an old Victorian house. What about the others in the rooms below, Roger and Mary? Surely they'd heard something? Then I remembered they were away; no one need ever know what I may or may not have heard. I got out of bed and attempted to look out the window without moving the curtain. I didn't want to be responsible; I didn't want to be a part of this. I didn't want this to be a part of me. I couldn't see a thing and the cries had stopped. Whatever it was, it was over and I turned to get back into bed. But then the woman's cry changed.

"My little boy, please, somebody help my little boy."

So it wasn't a rape – what was it? I could hear other voices too and I knew then that whatever was happening, it could happen without me. It was now out of my hands. I heard a siren – maybe the police? Police, ambulance, whatever; it was a siren to say go back to bed Gregory and don't worry about things that don't concern you. I felt sick but relieved. Sick at myself but relieved it was sorted without me. I learnt the next day that it had been a house fire and the woman's young baby had been killed. She wasn't a drunk, she wasn't being raped and her screams were for real.

A week or so later Mary read about it in the local paper.

"Did you see this?" she asked. "It's awful!"

I didn't tell her what I'd heard, that I lay in bed listening, doing nothing while something terrible happened to somebody else's world. Not my world though, not quite.

I only knew Mary and Roger so well because we'd been involved in the same accident; or rather, I'd watched as the car they were travelling in crashed. Roger had asked me to come along and play soccer and, as a passenger in the car behind, I saw everything as it happened. We were travelling at what, say 60mph, when the car in front of theirs hesitated and braked at the turn off the motorway. The choice was to crash or take their chances on the hard shoulder and, although they avoided hitting the car, the grass verge flipped them over through the air. I was distracted as we too were forced to brake hard. I sat blankly, in shock I guess, and stunned that I might have just seen the death of my new-found friends. The car that had caused the accident then drove away, oblivious to the chaos left behind.

Mary was sat in the front passenger seat with her safety belt fastened; when the car righted itself and hit an embankment some distance away, she escaped with heavy bruising. The driver too was strapped in but because of the age of the car there were no seat belts in the back. Roger was thrown hard across the back seat and broke his shoulder against the side of the car. It took a while to find the fourth passenger who had been thrown from the car and was lying in a nearby ditch with a broken back. At the hospital, once I knew that Roger and Mary would be OK, my sympathy went out to this fourth passenger – but not that much sympathy because I can't recall his name or even if he ever recovered.

Oh well, I think, I heard nothing last night. At least, this fire happened without me.

I call Tomas in from Suzie's for his tea.

The first thing Tomas asks is when is his Mum coming home and of course I say she's coming straight home from work. I always give Tomas something to eat early. He's not the biggest eater in the world and this way if he has anything with us later then OK, but if not then that's OK too. So our little routine is: Tomas eats, we play for a while or I tidy up a little, I cook for us all, dinner, an hour's telly and then bed for Tomas.

This evening Tomas and I play out in the street, taking turns with a ball trying to hit the opposite kerb, until I'm more concerned with watching for Caitlin to arrive home. The cold January day is coming to an end. It's good to enjoy the evening daylight before the darkness comes down, even if it is only just after five when we decide to quit. It would have been nice for Caitlin to walk round the corner and see us playing but I reach the point where I'm prolonging the game just for this one moment that's never going to happen.

I give Caitlin's office a ring before five-thirty but the call goes through on to the nightline, as though there's no one left around to answer. I only ring to suggest she comes home immediately and not to get caught up in some case she feels obliged to complete. When there's no answer to my call it seems to confirm that she's on her way.

So where is she and why hasn't she called? I already know something's not quite right and if I'm honest then I guess Tomas does too. When it's obvious she's not about to join us to eat then I have to make out it's no big deal. If I'd known I could have pretended to Tomas that Caitlin called earlier, while he was next door with Suzie, but he knows she hasn't and he wants to know why. He's not worried; it's just a break from routine so he needs an explanation.

We sit down to eat and I'm straight with him.

"I think your Mum went for a drink after work," I say. "If she had a tough day then she probably fancied a pint."

"Are you mad at her?" asks Tomas and I smile.

"No," I say, "it's fine." And in a way it is but Tomas has picked up on my concern, based not on whether Caitlin has gone to the pub but on the past week coming back at us. I don't believe for one minute we're free of it and sitting here alone with Tomas is a long way from Caitlin's 'the earliest I can get away' of this lunchtime.

Lunchtime, teatime, bed time. It's times like this I wish my reactions were more in line with the rest of humanity; any change from the norm and I never know how to act. Tomas and I do the usual evening things together but all the time, and particularly as I put him to bed, there's the question in the air between us – when will my Mum be home? Only by brushing it off and making light of it do I get him to settle at all, stressing the need for sleep and school tomorrow.

"I'll get your Mum to give you a kiss goodnight when she comes in, OK? She won't be very late or else she'd have phoned by now." I convince Tomas but as I leave him to sleep I've yet to convince myself. It is unusual for Caitlin not to call. I sit in the living room and try to think what she could be up to; try not to think what else she could be up to. Is it really so simple as the need for a drink and some space from the house? Is she looking for a break from Tomas and myself? Or is it just me she can't stand?

When I'm alone in the house with Tomas, I tend to see things clearly for what they are. This usually amounts to seeing what jobs need doing and getting on with them and sure enough, I start clearing away toys, but then I stop and think, what the fuck? I often enjoy time alone while Tomas is tucked up in bed but tonight there's no avoiding it; this thing is going to beat us, Caitlin and I. This lunchtime was OK, I was beginning to get through to her and we were reaching some sort of normality but then something happens and we're back to this. Or is this a good thing? If she'd had as bad a day as she claimed she was having, then maybe the pub is the best place for her to get it out her system. Phoning me is probably the last thing on her mind. But who is she with?

I walk through to the bedroom and check – no suitcases missing. Fucking stupid! I hate this Mad Detective stuff, looking for clues when there's nothing to be found. I sit down on the bed and try to think what she could be up to. I remember how before I lived with Caitlin I would try to judge from the bedclothes if she'd slept with someone the night before. (As I say, the Mad Detective.) Did I really think her suitcase would be missing? She'd used that case when she finally ran away from Immy. Imran. Standing on the platform at Leeds station, alone with her case, waiting on the train back to Manchester. Why do I remember that as though I were there?

We only have the two suitcases anyway. We each brought one from our previous lives. The larger of the two is mine and it's the case I used to carry my entire belongings when I moved in with Caitlin. (Tomas said I could stay so long as I brought all my friends, though he later changed that to on condition that I became his Dad.) I pull my suitcase down from the top of the wardrobe. There are still a few things in here and only recently Caitlin suggested that I deliberately keep them hidden. This was on a par with the diary episode and I thought – this is not the person I knew when I first met Caitlin. It's as though I'm suddenly held to account for things that were previously of no importance. Her reasoning is sound, I suppose: these belongings could appear to have been hidden away but really, what are we coming to when she thinks of me in this way? Maybe you see now why I like to think of her busy at work, getting pissed in the pub? The sooner we get back to normal life the better; we haven't fucked each other since our visit to the hospital.

Most of it is junk in the suitcase – not much to show for my life before we met. I can't imagine why I've kept it. There are several homemade signs of destinations from my hitching days. Leeds, Manchester, York, London – no secrets here. An old pair of glasses I once wore – I try them on and look in the mirror and see why I changed to contacts. My collection of oil paints that I'm saving for Tomas when he's old enough to use them (and when no doubt they'll have gone hard in the tubes). There's a bicycle lamp with leaking batteries. All these things – they aren't what Caitlin is talking about. There are letters in here too, scraps of paper with scribbled messages that I've wanted keeping. And why shouldn't I keep them? I'm not about to disregard the first twenty-three years of my life just because I've lived with Caitlin for the past two. These scraps still hold an interest for me; I wouldn't be the person I am now unless these things had happened to me.

So why hide them away Gregory? I hear Caitlin ask.

I realise I want her to come home even if she is going crazy.

I have to laugh! The first note I pick up is a card from Caitlin saying 'You must be mad'. I must be mad for choosing to be with her. I want to show it to her: see, do you remember writing this? And together we'd think back to the exact time soon after we first met, when Caitlin couldn't believe I was interested in her, couldn't imagine that I'd want to take on so much. I didn't see things that way; I just knew that I wanted her. I'm not saying I didn't think twice about Tomas, because I did, but once I met him I couldn't help but love him. And still Caitlin refused to believe. One evening we were alone together once Tomas was asleep.

"I think you should go," said Caitlin.

"You mean you want me to go home?"

"Yes."

"Why?" I tried to think what I could have said or done that was so wrong.

"I just think you should go," said Caitlin. "I don't think this will work."

"Are you finishing with me?" This after seeing each other for several weeks; we were already lovers. I thought everything was fine. Things were more than fine; I was already in love with her.

"Once you get to know me properly then you won't want me anymore," said Caitlin. "I'd rather just finish it now."

"Don't you think I should make up my own mind about that?"

"There are things you won't like."

"So tell me."

She said nothing for a moment.

"Just go, will you?"

"No, not like this."

She shrugged. I stood there like a prick.

"Are you telling me to leave?" I asked. "Because if you are then I have to go." Still she said nothing. "But I don't want to," I said.

I stayed. I wanted her. I wanted to look after her. She was anaemic and I used to cook dinners of liver and spinach, anything to help build her up. I chopped wood for the fire and made sure the flat was warm when she came in from work. I collected Tomas from nursery so she could earn more money. I worked on the flat. Whatever I did, I did because I wanted to be with her. For some reason I knew: everything in my life up until that point was as though I was just waiting to be with Caitlin.

She reminded of a stray kitten we'd saved at home years ago – there was nothing to this cat and you could push her over with just a touch of your finger. Even as an adult, the cat was never well, always weak and sick. But of all the pets that came and went, this one was the real survivor. Some nights with Caitlin, we'd be making love and she would become desperate for me, lying on her side with me behind her, reaching back to urge me on, harder and harder, not that I was being so gentle anyway, but she would hit me until I too lost myself and grabbed her so hard that I feared she might break; but she didn't.

And the card she wrote to me, telling me I must be mad – if I'd thrown it in the bin, then what? Would we ever remember how we felt? These notes, these other letters – what sense is there to me without them? I need these things to remind me who I am. I'm a writer, for Christ's sake, I need to write these things down and having written them down then I need to keep them. What do I amount to if all I am is some sad sap waiting for Caitlin to come home from the pub?

There's a copy of a letter I wrote to a girl called Brenda, written in long hand. Even back then I realised I had to write things down to remember, so I wrote to Brenda and then I wrote out a copy. I knew I never wanted to forget how I felt at that time. Brenda had decided to stop seeing me for fear of becoming pregnant. 'I hate people who control their feelings,' I wrote. 'I don't give a damn for your sensible decisions ...' Etcetera. Now I can look back on both – her decision and my letter – and think of it all as something of a joke or a lesson learnt. But I can remember it. Come to think of it now, it's an even better joke than I knew – we could have been enjoying as much risk free sex as we liked.

I was eighteen at the time so Brenda would have just turned seventeen, clever, smart and sexy. I don't mind telling you I loved her and believe also that she loved me. This one fact still gives me pause for thought because Brenda's love was a love worth having. She could be irritatingly logical but once she'd thought something through then you valued her decision. And this at seventeen! You can imagine that the love of such a person is not so easy to come by and not a thing to be taken lightly. When we started sleeping together it was at the risk, we thought, of Brenda becoming pregnant. Time after time we went ahead with it in the full knowledge that perhaps this time we wouldn't be so lucky. Now you might say that this doesn't really go with the picture I've painted of sensible Brenda and you'd be right but we'd reached a point where the need to fuck each other was stronger than any other consideration. One night in particular I remember Brenda coming into my room when I was staying over and the layout of the rooms was such that we must have had sex only inches away from her mother's head. Maybe this was the occasion Brenda decided she had to put a stop to things, I don't know. I do know that neither of us wanted an accident on our hands, but of the two of us only Brenda had the nerve to call it off. I was very bitter at the time, hence the letter, but you get over these things. I have the letter though, or at least a copy of it, and I shall always know what it meant to be Gregory at that time.

And now, now what do I think? I wonder if we'd ever heard of contraception. I think it's funny that Brenda will never know she was trying to prevent an accident that could never have happened. And I'm not bitter about it at all. (And if I'm really honest – painfully honest – I remember that possibly the real reason for Brenda finishing with me was that as I moved away to college in Manchester, I started going with other girls, and Brenda more than likely heard about it. But that last bit wasn't in the letter so it doesn't count. Oh yes, this was Gregory all right; this was the real me.)

Also in the suitcase I have a note from Leta saying 'Thanks for being just the way you are. Love you and missing you. Take care, Leta.' When I read it now I can recall exactly where I first read it and how it made me feel. That doesn't necessarily mean I want to return to those days but I enjoy remembering it all the same. I have a letter from when Leta and I had fallen out. 'Gregory, why don't you hate me? What a stupid question, I think the answer is because you love and understand me in a way – God! I don't ever want to lose you, you know. I can't apologise for what I have done, there's nothing I could do to change what I would be apologising for. The last thing I want to do is to hurt you, I would rather be without you than hurt you anymore. My body feels wretched and ugly without you ...'

What was I to do with a letter such as that? Well, I know what I did and it helps explain who I am and what I'm doing now. What I'm saying is that memory adds meaning to my life, rather than it being one perpetual present, one repeating accident. These notes and letters fill in some of the blanks where my memory fails.

There is one thing here I can't figure out, however hard I try to remember. I stare at this scrap of paper and try to decipher what it means:

1331 – dinner times
1281 – Sat & 1 day
1243 – 4 days
1132 – to be arr.
– 13 hours
1458 –

The note's in my handwriting and I can guess it dates from 1979 but beyond this I haven't a clue what I was telling myself. I've always held on to the note; I know it doesn't really matter but it irritates the hell out of me that I could have written something that I wouldn't later understand. Obviously some schedule I was setting myself, like Gatsby, and I can feel the sense of hoped-for self-improvement – but what? I have the note but what it means is lost to me, I can read the words but I can't reach back to when they were written.

I place the letters back in the suitcase along with the rest of the junk. Why don't I throw this stuff away? Isn't it time I moved on? The one concession I make is the bike lamp with the leaking batteries; I throw them in the bin. I remember the diary in the drawer and yes, there it is; I thought Caitlin might have thrown it out. I think about what I have: a handful of letters, a few scraps of paper and a diary kept for three months. How else do people remember their days? Photographs – I have a few photographs but they don't tell me how I felt. They illustrate the occasions they were taken, they help I suppose but Christ! I'm only twenty-five and already I can't remember most of the things that have happened to me.

Maybe this really is all I amount to – sitting alone going through an old diary, thinking of old girlfriends and minding my current girlfriend's child?

Where the fuck is Caitlin and why hasn't she called?

Caitlin O'Connor is standing on a platform in Leeds City Station. The train to Manchester is there in front of her and due to depart in three minutes. She has a ticket – a single ticket – for a journey that will take just an hour to go across, over and through the mountains separating the two cities. Her suitcase is on the platform next to her feet and it contains all she thought fit to bring, mainly clothes and cosmetics, no real possessions as such. The train has just pulled into the station and, in their rush to leave the train, the evening commuters from York push their way through the passengers waiting on the platform. The station is busy also with the Leeds rush-hour commuters, impatient with passengers such as Caitlin who slow them down with their baggage and their uncertainty. Who would choose to travel at such a time?

Regular travellers circle around Caitlin – if they get stuck behind her there's no way a seat will be free (although given her shape and size, it's fairly certain somebody will give up their seat). It's not that Caitlin is unsure which is the correct train; no, it's more that she's unsure about her decision to actually board the train. Because although the train goes to Manchester, and Caitlin knows that this is where she wants to go, she doesn't know what to do once she arrives. She has no destination beyond Manchester Piccadilly Station, no place to go to, no person to call. If she leaves Leeds then all she has are the contents of her suitcase. Whatever cash she has was spent on the taxi into town and then the train ticket. Such was her hurry to leave this afternoon she forgot her savings book but anyway, what use would be? The savings are in their joint names and it requires both their signatures to withdraw any money and, here's another problem, the father of the baby inside her is the husband she's trying to leave. She doesn't know if she can do this on her own.

The guard walks along the train, slamming each door shut as he makes his way to the rear of the train. As he reaches the last carriage – Caitlin's carriage if she was to board the train – he hesitates before closing the final door.

"Are you wanting this train, love?" he asks Caitlin.

She shakes her head, no, and he slams this door too and walks past Caitlin to his own compartment, blowing his whistle for the train to leave. No last minute dramatic boarding of the train for Caitlin, not in her condition, and the train pulls away to leave her alone on the empty platform. She checks the monitor above her head – there's another train in an hour. She still has her ticket; she could still leave. Caitlin picks up her suitcase – it's awkward more than heavy – and she follows the departed train along the platform, if only for something to do rather than make a decision. It would be nice to think things through as she walks but she can't get the thoughts clear in her head. The obvious facts are too obvious to consider, the arguments for and against leaving too familiar for Caitlin to go over again. It's just the resolution she lacks. At the end of the platform, at the barrier to prevent her walking down the slope to the tracks, she watches as the train to Manchester disappears from view. She traces the track on which it had travelled, again as far as she can see, trying to make out the workings of the many junctions and cross-junctions of a station the size of Leeds. She's distracted by the movement of other trains arriving and departing and soon loses sight of which track would have taken her to Manchester.

She looks down at the suitcase by her feet (she would have looked at her feet if she could see them) and cries. She hates these tears because they betray her; she has so little control over so many different parts of her body these days and these tears are just another disloyal act of a disloyal body. She wants to be strong but she's not, not in mind or in body. She knows what she must do but doesn't know how to do it. She guesses that other people go home to their parents but Caitlin can't do this; her parents are alive and in Manchester but she can't go home. Who cares whether it's they that can't forgive her or she that can't go back? It amounts to the same thing – her life has led her to this point, this platform, and the barrier at the end of this platform. She lets the tears fall – why not?

Caitlin made her decisions three years ago and she knows it – that's why there are none to be made today. She's in the train station of what feels like a foreign city because she decided to marry and live with Imran, against her parents' wishes, and in the sure knowledge she would lose all her friends. Yes, it was love but there was something much more in there too – a rejection of a whole way of thinking, of a mindset that said you keep to your own. Imran was just too different; a different colour, a different race, a different set of beliefs. Too much for Caitlin's parents, her brothers, her sister (even her sister), too much for them to accept because it was all too different from what they knew. This was her family in the privacy of their home, before they even considered the reaction of their friends, their neighbours, and their church. And Caitlin, young and in love, who saw only a set of values she was beginning to abhor, considered them so wrong that she didn't give a second thought to leaving them behind for good.

Perhaps more than all these things, it was Imran himself she loved, still loves. She knows that beautiful is not the right word to describe a man but beautiful is what he is. His every movement, his grace, his looks and his gentleness – she loves these things in Imran. And still she believes in him; standing here crying alone, she refuses to let the bad things justify her family's ignorance. She'll never go back to their world and allow them to believe they were right because they were wrong, so wrong wrong wrong, and are still so wrong, and so what if this is all Caitlin has – they'll never be right.

This is all Caitlin has. If Imran was her means of escape

from a world she was only too pleased to leave behind, there's no going back on the choices she made. He was her ticket away from Manchester; he had money, he loved her and they could be together. Now all she has is a paper ticket back to Manchester; might that city now be as strange to her as here? She certainly doesn't know anyone in Manchester. At least here in Leeds she has her home and any hope of a future. Caitlin accepts it – she has nowhere to go but home to Imran and yes, he'll be home by now and wanting to know where she might be. And she's going to turn up with her suitcase that will tell him what he already knows and then Caitlin will know too well what she's done, or at least what she's been trying to do.

She takes the ticket from her pocket and places it in her purse, picks up her suitcase and retraces her steps along the platform and then to the exit of the station. She has no money for a cab; she may have enough for a bus but she hasn't the first idea of where a bus would go from. In the two years that she's lived here, she hasn't even learnt where the bus station is. She knows Headingley and she knows the way home from town but she's been leading an oddly sheltered and unreal life, not wanting for anything and never worrying where Imran's money comes from. In fact, not until this moment has the matter of money concerned Caitlin in all the time she's been with Imran. She's worked at gradually improving their already beautiful home to be ready – not for her to be alone with her suitcase in Leeds City Station, but for when she becomes the mother of their children together. This is what she wanted and now this is all she has.

Caitlin decides to make her way out of town using the only route she knows and then, hopefully, to catch a bus going in the right direction. She knows the way up from the station, past the Town Hall and the University. It's a hell of a walk just to get out of town but Caitlin doesn't mind; if she's walking it gives her the illusion of activity over indecision. She could ask for directions to the bus station but she doesn't trust herself to approach a passer-by without breaking down in tears. She feels as though everything is writ upon her face as it is. Her attempt to hide the swelling above her eye with dark glasses is a dead giveaway now that the late winter afternoon has turned to dusk. The glasses fool no one, she knows, and look so odd they suggest this specific injury to be much worse than it actually is. Also, the thought of negotiating the bus station at rush hour, of having to ask again for the number of the bus and at which bus stop to stand – it all seems way too much to do without losing control and breaking down. It's this fear more than any other, of making a public display of herself, that persuades Caitlin the walk out of town is her best possible option, however arduous and exhausting it may prove to be.

She picks up her suitcase once again and, ignoring the line of taxis along the curved front of the station that thought her a safe bet for a fare, begins to make her way against the flow of people rushing to catch their evening train. She knows she must look quite unusual. Heavily pregnant with a winter coat that won't fasten across her stomach, carrying a suitcase but walking away from the station, her dark Greta Garbo glasses and, too late she now realises, no hat to protect her from the cold snow flurries that are carried along on the wind. She has no umbrella and besides, she'd probably be unable to manage one without it blowing away. She puts her suitcase down once more, this time to the side of the pavement against the wall of the station building, and she unfastens the clasps. Lifting the lid of the case, she finds what she's looking for and then fashions a headscarf to cover her ears, tying a knot beneath her chin. The fastening on the suitcase is difficult to do without kneeling on the case and positioning the catch just so. Once this is done she leans on the case to help her stand and is again set to start her walk out of town. Every step she takes, Caitlin is conscious of the glances of people walking by. Many are too preoccupied to notice but those that do take a second look as the oddness registers and those with better intentions think of offering to help. It only takes a second though, or maybe even less, for them to think better of it; she could be going anywhere and it's best not to get involved.

Caitlin is pleased when she gets through the train commuters and away from the station, and pleased again to be away from the well-lit shopping areas, making her way across The Headrow and up along the side of the Town Hall. Here at least is some anonymity and fewer questioning looks. The effort of simply walking is exhausting and the weight of the case is beginning to tell on her shoulders and lower back. The periods between stopping to change hands and taking a rest become shorter and shorter each time. She feels so useless when she considers that this is the best she can do; this is as far as her little rebellion has carried her. How quickly she's been reduced to this pathetic state, walking home in the cold and unable to carry the few belongings she considered worth taking. She could have been at home in the warmth, sharing a meal with Immy, her feet raised to help the circulation in her legs. Her beautiful house – how could she have left her beautiful house? And left it for this?

Caitlin begins to seriously doubt if she can make it much further. She seems to have misjudged her direction, or at least the direction of the out-of-town traffic. Somehow she needs to be further over to the right, to get on to Woodhouse Lane in the hope of maybe catching the right bus home. As the road crosses over the motorway she further doubts her sense of direction but then she sees the hospital and knows again where she is. The thought of just presenting herself at the hospital occurs to her – but to say what?

"I'm sorry but I can't get home?"

Maybe if they saw the bruising they would allow her to stay? Surely they would consider the welfare of her baby? The idea of somebody taking control, of just being taken care of, clean sheets and safety – Caitlin feels a rush of wanting and again the tears flow but she walks on past the lights of the hospital. There would be questions and possibly the police and she knows she couldn't go through with that. She couldn't confront Immy, couldn't take sides with strangers against the man who, despite everything, she loves. Her one chance had been to run far away, to completely disappear, and this she's been unable to do.

As she makes her way on to Woodhouse Lane, a bus passes by and Caitlin knows she's finally in the right place to find her way home. She sees a bus stop ahead and struggles the short distance in the knowledge that at least here she can rest. She checks the details posted at the stop and figures it shouldn't be too long before another bus comes along, which is just as well because she feels exposed and alone. There's no shortage of traffic passing her by but very few pedestrians and certainly no other passengers waiting. After the exertion of her walk, Caitlin has built up a sweat but now the cold finds her and she holds the front of her coat closed around her. A bus arrives but as she holds out her hand she sees Out of Service as the destination and it drives straight past, followed by a gust of wind that whips her coat open once more. She sees a second bus at the bottom of the hill, picking up passengers from the previous stop and, as it makes its way up to Caitlin, she makes out Headingley on the front and again sticks her hand out for it to stop. As the doors open, she struggles with the suitcase before asking the driver how much to Headingley.

"Which part?"

She finds it hard to describe where she needs to get off, agreeing instead with the driver's first suggestion and feeling relief when she sees she has enough to pay. The bus moves off and Caitlin very nearly takes a fall but by kicking her foot against the suitcase and steadying herself on the arm of another passenger, she manages then to grab a hand rail in time. She apologises to the other passenger. There's no way she can lift the case on to the luggage rack so she remains standing, with her foot against the case to keep it upright. She's grateful no one offers her a seat because what then would she do with her case? She closes her eyes in the hope it makes her invisible but knows all too well she's not. Her glasses, her belly and her headscarf all mark her out as different. She senses the eyes of everyone in the bus upon her. Caitlin can feel the sweat on her forehead, as much from embarrassment as from the physical effort of the walk and she curses again at having put herself through this. Behind her glasses, she keeps her eyes tightly closed until fear of missing her stop makes her check the darkness outside for recognisable landmarks. It's difficult to make anything out, even when the bus stops to let passengers off, so it seems to Caitlin she must have missed Headingley completely. Panicking, she rings the bell for the next stop and only then recognises the shopping centre. Floods of relief wash over her as other passengers get off; she would rather have walked than tell the driver she pressed the button by mistake.

Two further stops and Caitlin is once again in the night air. She was briefly tempted to leave the suitcase on the bus because now she's close to home – and she has made it home, against all the odds she has made it – there's a whole new scenario to face that may be better without the evidence of a suitcase full of clothes. Might it be possible to pretend? If she walked in without the case, is there a chance that Immy might not notice? Is there a credible reason for her not being at home? Could she be breezy and chatty and light-hearted, could she tease Immy for not remembering she'd arranged to – to do what? To go see some friends – which friends are these? No, not a hope, there's not a hope of fooling Imran; having made it home, having decided to come home after having decided to leave her home, Caitlin must now face up to whatever may await her.

Imran takes the case from her hand without saying a word.

Diary 1982

January 1ˢᵗ – If I have one New Year resolution, then it's to finish my story. The end is in sight but I want to give it a biting edge so that each little episode counts.

Jan 5ᵗʰ – Finished the major chapters. First section needs re-writing. It gets easier the closer I get to finishing.

Jan 6ᵗʰ – This diary has lasted six days, making it the longest diary I've ever kept.

Jan 8ᵗʰ – Have only the end of my story to write – maybe I'm in too much of a hurry? Reported in The Times today that blocks of ice were floating down York High Street and that two York schoolgirls were the only pupils to get to school – by reindeer! OK, so it's cold but people are getting carried away.

Jan 9ᵗʰ – Wrote a little of the book. It seems to be writing itself.

Jan 10ᵗʰ – A woman's lips froze to her car door as she was blowing into the lock to de-frost it (Daily Mail). Water has been freezing on ducks' backs and the fish caught in the North Sea are coming up ready-frozen (Daily Mail again).

Jan 11ᵗʰ – Minus 32C in Chicago – now that's cold.

Jan 12ᵗʰ – Re-typing early part of the book – it's boring and depressing.

Jan 13ᵗʰ – Very dejected about my book.

Jan 14ᵗʰ – Feeling very highly-strung about my book. I want to make people feel when they read it. When I came upstairs to bed just now, I looked through the whole of the story and had incredible faith in it.

Jan 17ᵗʰ – Did very little. Typed a few pages. Only in the last fifty pages or so does anything happen, but then the story is short.

Jan 18ᵗʰ – A letter from Leta, saying all the gang are getting back together again; will I be I around? Finished typing my book.

Jan 19ᵗʰ – Calling my book Faulty Wiring; bad wiring in the house and in the people too. Written off to nine publishers, asking if they would read my book.

Jan 26ᵗʰ – Met Leta for a drink, acted like an idiot, probably with waiting so long to see her. Oh well…

Jan 28ᵗʰ – Got approached in Moss Side precinct by a junkie asking for 10p to buy some speed maaan!

Jan 29ᵗʰ – Changed into my suit, went into town to meet Leta, Mike etc. They weren't there in the foyer as arranged, eventually found them upstairs where Leta said she'd forgotten. Talked to Leta on my own for a while. The evening was supposed to be a grand reunion but it was never going to work – it's obvious Mike is still cut up over Leta while she pretends that everything's fine.

Feb 2nd – Met Leta. Told me about her and Sutcliffe – what kind of a name is that? I couldn't understand why she called him by his surname but then I figured it out – it's his first name! Purely bed partners, she said. Wishes we'd all just give him a chance – like that's going to happen! Told me all she thought about marriage, boyfriends etc., that she'd forget Sutcliffe if she met the right person – right, I thought.

When I told her about my writing, she said her real father in the States made his money from writing but didn't enjoy it, only did it for the money. I wish I had that problem!

I feel very awkward with her and act it. I can't figure her out, not what I expected at all. I only ever knew her as Mike's girlfriend and that seems such a long time ago. Maybe it'll sort itself out, who knows?

Feb 3rd – Went to the laundrette and two women had a fight over who was next in line for the dryer, fists and everything. Better than the telly!

Feb 4th – Met Leta.

Feb 5th – Met Leta.

Feb 6th – No replies from publishers – chose the wrong publishers, it seems I'm not thinking or acting like a writer.

Feb 9th – Met Leta.

Feb 10th – Met Leta at Piccadilly Station, went for a drink and then a meal, took Leta home and then ran for my bus. Went straight to bed, woke up two hours later feeling like shit!

Feb11th – Leta rang to thank me for last night.

Feb 12th – Leta was supposed to ring but didn't. Saw her later and she said she'd forgotten. Forgotten??

Feb 22nd – Leta stayed here. Very tense at first but it was good, very good.

Feb 25th – Leta stayed. She makes me feel I'm worth something, she reacts when I touch her. When we make love, I look her in the face; her eyes are like a wild animal. I hope she's not lying to me. There's no reason why she should be lying, only I want to hear it so much I can barely believe it when I hear her.

March 3rd – Impossible to retain an air of impartiality with Leta. I'm scared of letting go, even though I know it's the one way to be happy. Who wants to be hurt? Letting go puts you in a hurtable position.

March 8th – Reading The Tin Drum. Where do you get an imagination like that?

March 9th – Laziness – if I wanted to write then I would make the time for it.

March 10th – If I'm going to get hurt then I'm going to get hurt. If she wants to run rings around me then she can. Still heard nothing back from any publishers but sent off my book to one of them anyhow – first constructive thing I've done in nearly two months.

What the fuck is happening to me?

March 11th – Looked at Writers' and Artists' Yearbook – anything you could possibly do wrong in submitting a manuscript then I've done it. Leta stayed.

March 26th – Leta's parents' silver wedding party. Sutcliffe was there – not so detached as I'd like to think.

March 27th – Leta came round. We made love, had a bath and felt better about things but there's still something there.

March 29th – Last night spoilt by my not being able to cope with the situation. Leta says to trust her. I'm very, very unhappy about it all.

March 30th – Leta stayed.

April 1st – Went with Leta to court where she was the witness to an accident. Bought food together and Leta cooked. Had a bath and made love before going out, fell asleep together when we finally got to bed – perfect.

April 2nd – I stayed in bed after Leta left for work but couldn't sleep. All I'm interested in is making love and being with Leta.

April 4th – Leta's Mum was to cook us a meal but during the afternoon we heard Sutcliffe had a relapse of TB from his days in India. The doctor said to move Sutcliffe from his damp flat so Leta took him home and I missed out on my meal. I wish the cunt would fuck off back to India and die! Leta came round at about 10.00pm, pretty pissed off. Eventually we both snapped out of it. I've never wanted anyone as consistently as I do Leta.

April 8th – Must get back that blind necessity to write, to the exclusion of all else.

I put the diary with the letters and scraps of paper in the suitcase and lift the case up next to Caitlin's. Not so outrageous after all, is it? Not sufficient a reason to suppose that because things aren't too good between Caitlin and myself that I'd consider getting back in touch with Leta. I know I don't want to see Leta again but Caitlin isn't thinking rationally; she sees words written years ago and applies them to the here and now. Caitlin believes I'm still addicted to Leta, she believes I've never really shaken free of an addiction that is as harmful to me as any drug could be. I have no contact with Leta yet I seem to remember her with an apparent longing that must be addiction. Knowing that she damaged me, knowing that ultimately Leta was no good and yet still wanting her – surely these are the classic symptoms of addiction?

If only I had a diary to show Caitlin how I freed myself of the drug that was Leta, maybe then she'd believe me? Before Leta I was addicted to Brenda but there's no diary for back then, just a sad letter of abuse. Maybe I'm addicted to Caitlin now, who knows? I've yet to try living without her to test how strong my addiction would be.

"Where are you going?"

Jesus – it's Tomas! Twice now he's come through and seen

me going through my stuff. He must have seen me with the suitcase. He has this habit of just standing silently behind you, or when you're asleep in bed he waits so that you sense him before you eventually come to. I don't know whether it's the quiet or his dark, almost black eyes but it's unnerving.

"I'm not going anywhere," I say.

"What time is it?" he asks but it's a trick question – what he means is it's past the time I said his mother would be home.

"She'll be here soon," I say. "The pubs are closed now so she can't be much longer." I lead him back to his room and tuck him into bed but this restlessness is so unlike Tomas that it's difficult to reassure him. "I'll tell her to come in and kiss you goodnight." This is the second time I've promised this tonight.

"What if she doesn't come home?"

"She'll be here, you'll see. Now, come on, back to sleep. You have school in the morning."

I kneel by the side of his bed and my presence soon helps him return to sleep. I don't know what I shall say if he wakes up again. He's put his trust in me and I don't know if that trust is justified. I've told him not to worry but now I know there is a reason to worry and if Caitlin isn't home by the morning then there'll be no hiding it from Tomas. I shall have to tell him – what?

I move away slightly from the bed, not wishing to wake him, but I don't leave the room. Tomas and I have come a long way in a short space of time and this thing will test the strength of what we have between us. What did he think when I came along, suddenly having to share his Mum? There was no way I could have carried on seeing Caitlin without taking on some responsibility for Tomas and we were lucky in that it seemed to suit us both from an early stage. I didn't go ahead lightly but even so I had no idea just how attached, and how quickly attached, I would become. I've spent my adult life learning how to detach myself from relationships – fifty ways to leave your lover and all that – but nothing prepared me for the commitment I was to make with Tomas. From the early fun we had together to a growing responsibility, to finding the correct balance between the two, with no shortage of mistakes along the way – I was his friend and then I became his Dad.

Is this how kids get messed up? I can't imagine how he'll react in the morning if Caitlin's not here – is this all it takes? Tomas is so sweet-natured, so accepting of his lot in life when he's more reason than most kids not to be. When I think back to what I got up to – though granted not at Tomas's age – I can't imagine this beautiful boy of ours becoming anything like me. It wasn't just the stealing; I used to love the thrill of sticking pencil refills into an electric socket for example and touching the lead with my fingers. At first it was just curiosity, to see what might happen if I – whoa! I was thrown back into the room, astonished at all that power travelling along such a little strip of lead. My teeth were on edge and I felt sick but these were nothing compared to the buzz of electricity running through my body. I knew it was dangerous and I knew it was wrong but it was something I had to try again. I wanted to fully appreciate the rush as the electricity made its way through me to earth. There was a moment of panic as the lead stuck to my fingers and I thought enough for now – that was too scary by far.

A cousin of mine liked to hold his breath until he passed out. He wanted to find out what would happen, that was all. His parents would find him alone in his room, blue in the face and refusing to breathe. This was his passion, his addiction and yes, he grew out of it; my cousin's OK, he's happy. And Leta – whom Caitlin fears is my latest addiction, my latest compulsion – Leta was fucked by her uncle at the age of fourteen and had to have the baby aborted. Fourteen! She lives and works; you'd never know that such a thing ever happened to her or her family. They get by, they're doing fine.

But how do I protect Tomas from these things; how do I keep the world from my little boy?

I leave Tomas and turn off the lights. I have to do something so I telephone Ann, Caitlin's best friend from the office. Although she's a workmate, Ann is close enough to know what we've been through over the past week or so.

Neither are great lovers of office life and Ann would have the low-down on anything that may have happened at work today. Ann is slightly older than Caitlin and me; it seems appropriate to call her. The phone rings for quite a while and I know I'm getting her out of bed.

"Ann, it's Gregory."

"Just give me a second – "

"I know it's late, I'm sorry."

"Give me a second and I'll be with you." I can hear Ann put down the receiver and draw up a chair. She's in no rush and in a way this composes me. She must know I'm phoning about Caitlin and I feel I've picked the right person to call. "Is she in a bad way?" she asks.

"She's not even here, Ann. She never came home after work. What happened to her this afternoon?"

"It's nearly one o'clock, Gregory."

"I know." What Ann means is, why leave it so late to start calling? "I met her at lunchtime and she said she was going to leave early and to come straight home. Did something happen this afternoon for her to change her mind?"

"Plenty happened this afternoon. Did she not phone? What did you think when she didn't come home?"

"That she'd had a bad day and gone to the pub," I say.

"Weren't you worried?"

"No, I thought maybe it was a good thing to do, get something out her system. I just wish she'd called." Jesus, how can I say that Caitlin is better off out drinking than being at home with me? But that's the fact of it, that's what we've come to and it seems to have taken no time at all. I leave it hanging in the air; Ann can take from that what she likes. She's silent on the other end of the phone.

"I'm sorry, Gregory," she says after a moment, "I didn't mean to suggest you'd been thoughtless. If she went for a drink after work then I can't think who she would've gone with. Would she drink in a pub on her own?"

"Yes, but not all night. She either went with someone she knew or met someone there." (Met someone – it begins…)

Silence again as Ann takes this in.

"Caitlin was still in the office as I left," she says. "That was soon after five. I didn't see her to say goodbye but I'd seen her go into a private interview room shortly before I left and she didn't reappear after."

"What had happened to make her stay?"

"Like I said, plenty happened, but I've no idea what Caitlin was working on."

"She said something about some incident this morning?"

"No, that was cleared up immediately after lunch and came to nothing. She was working on some case and there was something about it. You know how it is at work when you get involved in something – perhaps she just became distracted?"

"No. I don't know." And I don't want to know either – employment, organisations – no thanks.

"Has she been very bad?" asks Ann.

"You mean at home? She's found it as hard as you'd expect."

"Do you think she came back to work too soon?"

"Not if she could be allowed to just get on with her work. She's been at home too long and besides, she couldn't really take much more leave without giving them a full explanation." I half expect Caitlin to walk in while I'm on the phone and give out to me for dragging Ann in on it. But there's nothing, no sound at the door to signal an end to this latest piece of shit. "I don't know what to do Ann," I say. Saying this makes me realise just how fucking lost I really am. "I'd go out and look for her but I can't leave Tomas. What should I do?"

"I think you're doing the right thing in staying there. We've got to presume she won't do anything stupid and that it's as you say, she just needs time on her own. Do you want me to have a drive around, see if I can spot her anywhere?"

"Christ no," I say. "You could drive all night and not see her. She must know what she's up to even if we don't."

"She's a big girl, Gregory."

"Yeah, but she's a crazy bitch!"

"I'll call you in the morning. Try to get some sleep."

Caitlin is crazy but I wonder just how crazy. Not Betty Blue type crazy, that's for sure. Not crazy enough to leave Tomas, definite. But tonight she's mad enough about something not to come home. She's stormed off before during some argument or other – haven't we all – but for Caitlin to stay out all night means she's hit an all-time low. And stay out where? Is she alone or is she with someone else? This thought brings me up sharp – I have no reason to be jealous but you don't always need a reason when the chaos is let loose in your mind.

She's had little comfort out of me lately. I regret now not trying harder to find the right words. It's not that I don't care, more that I can't find a way to reach her. Just the other day I went to put my arms around her but she shrugged me off.

"Get away from me, Gregory! There's only one thing you can do to make this OK and that's to get me pregnant!"

And then she steps back from the edge.

"Oh my God, what have I said? I'm so sorry, I didn't mean that…"

And so on. What am I to do? I think of Laurence Olivier and his justifying leaving Vivien Leigh, saying that no matter how much he loved her there was nothing more he could do to help her.

What if Caitlin's found comfort elsewhere, if she's hearing the right words from someone else?

I get undressed and into bed. I leave the hallway light on as always for Tomas but tonight it's also for Caitlin. I check the time – it's almost two – there's a chance she may have gone to a club and if so she would be in by three. It's going to be a long night. But I'm too tired to put myself through this again tonight, too tired to keep going over the same old ground and the same old fears, so I've no difficulty falling asleep. Exhaustion takes over.

It's not the falling asleep that's the problem; it's when I wake up an hour later that it really starts. I can be as cool as you like during the day but catch me alone now, with my senses working overtime and my mind racing through possibilities and probabilities, going over likely scenarios and equally unlikely explanations. Sure it's my head that's fucking me up, but it's my gut where I feel it most and I kneel on the bed, doubled over and holding my stomach.

As if the past week hasn't been bad enough, I now have this to face. Alone. I've been strong – I believe – for Caitlin but I've yet to really think through what this all means for me. I'm not going back to these three and then four in the morning nightmares of knowing that I'm here and she's somewhere else – because where Caitlin is wrong about Leta, so wrong, is here in these sheets. This is Leta's legacy to me – the loneliness, the doubt, the insecurity, and the knowledge that while I'm here alone then she most definitely is not. Don't talk to me about trust at four in the morning; you cling on to the hope that you're mistaken but you know you're right because it's always been this way, this is the way the world works, and once again you're the chump.

Face it Gregory, she's not coming home so what are your options? And I know right away what my options are – fuck all because Tomas is in the other bedroom and what am I going to do but stay? Where else would I go and what else do I have? This is it; swallow it.

Some time later, I'm not really sure of the time, I manage to fall back to sleep.

Three

The alarm sounds at seven, the time set for Caitlin to get up for work and way too early for Tomas to be up for school. At some point in the night he has climbed into bed with me and as I turn over I can see he's already wide-awake, waiting for me to come round. I smile and put my arms around him.

"When did you come in?"

"Last night," he says and it occurs to me that at the very moment I should have been awake, when Tomas needed me to be awake, I must have been fast asleep. I picture Tomas coming through, seeing me asleep, not seeing his Mum; how long did he have to stand there before finally deciding to get in?

"Did you go back to sleep?"

"I think so," he says. "She's not here, is she?"

"No, son, she's not." Any other time I'd be given the 'You lied to me' look but I can't describe the look Tomas is giving me now – hopeful, dependent? A 'tell me something good' look – but I've nothing good to tell him. We lie there together for a moment. He's so beautiful and perfect. "Your Mum never came home," I say. "I know I told you she would and I'm sorry; I really thought she would."

"Where do you think she is?"

"I don't know, Tomas, I really don't know."

"Mmm," he says.

"I'll be honest with you – "

"Are you going to level with me?"

"What?"

"Are you going to level with me, like Hannibal?" *The A-Team*.

"Yes," I smile, despite myself, "I'm going to level with you. I don't know what your Mum is doing; I don't know why she didn't come home last night. I saw her yesterday at lunchtime and I really thought she was OK. You know how upset she's been for the past week – "

"Why?"

"Why's she been upset?"

"Yes."

I think about this. Tomas knows we've been to the hospital on and off for the past few weeks. Happily – happily? – most of Caitlin's worse moments have been while Tomas was either at school or in bed so we've given him only the briefest of explanations for any outbursts of crying – not so much deliberately keeping him in the dark as keeping the weight of the world from his shoulders. I try to explain it as simply as I can. "The hospital told us that we couldn't have children together."

He thinks about this for a moment.

"You have me," he says.

"I know, and we couldn't ask for a nicer little boy" – he hugs me – "but you can't have any brothers or sisters, at least, not if me and your Mum stay together. This is what has been upsetting your Mum."

"And you think she got upset again yesterday."

"Yes, I guess so."

"Aren't you upset at all?" he asks.

"Yes, I am but everybody shows things in different ways."

"And are you going to stay together?"

Jesus, he doesn't miss a trick.

"Yes, I hope so."

"Why wouldn't my Mum want to come home?"

Simple question, obvious question; if she's hurting, if she's upset, then surely she'd want to be with the people she loves?

"I can't understand that either and this is where I'm going to level with you. I don't know where your Mum is and I don't know what she's thinking. If she needed time on her own – and we all do," I add as I see the look on Tomas' face, "if she needed time on her own then I wish she'd just asked. If she's gone to stay with a friend then I wish she'd called but if she's upset enough to stay away then I guess she's in no fit state to call."

"Do you think she got drunk?" Know your parents.

"Maybe," I say "and maybe she'll call before we leave for school." When I mention this I see the light in Tomas' eyes and I have to immediately dampen his hopes. "But if she was drunk then I doubt if she's awake yet, wherever she is."

I keep setting myself these traps to fall into. I'm not doing too well here; the problem is I'm as confused as Tomas and speaking as I'm thinking it through. I make a last attempt.

"OK," I say, "I'm going to concentrate on what we do know. However upset your Mum is, we know that she loves us and she knows that we love her. If she needs to do something like stay away from home for a few days then it's best that she does."

"Why?"

"Because in the end it will make things right again. And what we should do is to carry on as though everything's fine. That means having a wash, your breakfast, off to school and then home time this evening – we just have to trust that she's OK."

"What if she's had an accident?"

"And the other thing I was going to say was try not to worry – let me do the worrying. While you're at school I'll be phoning your Mum's work, things like that. We do what we can do, OK?" Tomas doesn't look too convinced.

"I want to stay here with you," he says.

"But your Mum may call to the school, we don't know." I brush the hair back from his forehead with my fingers. "Look, when I say don't worry I know you can't help but worry; your Mum's didn't come home last night." His face looks so lost, so helpless, when I say this. "But what I'm asking you to do is to be as grown up about it as you can, enough to accept that there's nothing we can do but wait. Imagining things like accidents won't help but being strong together will. There are two of us in this and we have to help each other out."

"Will she be back by the time I come home from school?"

he asks and then answers his own question. "We don't know, do we?"

"No, we don't know but I'll be there for you at home time and we agree together what to do then – OK?"

A moment's deliberation, but the appeal to being a grown up seems to work – as if that's such a great thing – and then he agrees. We shake on it *A-Team* style, thumb around thumb and a forearm-to-forearm grip.

There are no *Kramer v. Kramer* fiascos where breakfast is concerned for Tomas and I. We both know the drill and each other's limits too well at this time of the morning. Tomas will eat a little cereal. I'll ask him if he couldn't possibly eat some more, is he sure he's had enough, in the never-ending battle to get him to eat enough food. This will normally take place in the kitchen while his Mum is in the bathroom and if he can manage it then Tomas will always try to sneak back to his bedroom – not to sleep but to play. Caitlin leaving is usually the signal for Tomas to wash and dress; today we do all the same things only without her being around. Even this is not entirely unusual. There have been occasions when Caitlin wasn't here for some reason or other – away on a training course, away with friends for the weekend – and it's not unheard of for us to be alone together on a school morning. We both observe our pact to act normal. By eight-thirty it's time to leave; it's a good twenty-minute walk to Tomas' school, longer if he decides it's going to be a slow day. He insists on walking out past the burnt-out house and having a good look. We take our time – there are no other people around, no one else is gawking at the still-smouldering remains. It can't possibly still be on fire, so is that steam coming from the heat? Is it the cold chill of the morning, falling on the heat of the burnt-out rubble?

"What will happen to it now?" asks Tomas.

"I don't know, I guess it depends if they can rebuild the inside of the house." It's a miracle the houses next door weren't damaged, that the adjoining walls didn't buckle in the heat. We walk on and by the time we arrive at school it seems that Tomas will be fine. I talk things through with him one last time, just to be sure.

"I'm going to go to your Mum's office now," I say, "and then I'll try phoning her during the day. If she's not back by this evening then we'll phone some of your Mum's friends together."

But he's already switched modes and is focussed on being at school. We're past the kissing at the school gates stage so he runs and disappears into a playground full of children. I take this as a good sign that he's going to be OK.

"See you at home time," I call but he's gone, I don't even get an acknowledgement.

Caitlin's workplace is close by – hence the choice of school – and I walk over to the staff entrance. The office opens to the public at nine-thirty but they operate a flexi-time system so there's a distinct possibility Caitlin is already here. I know Frank the security guard from the days Caitlin and I would take Tomas to school together; he's an elderly guy and I always had the impression he approved of Caitlin's young man whenever we kissed goodbye by the door.

"Frank," I say and immediately I realise he's not sure who I am but as I mention Caitlin's name then he places me. He would only know me as Caitlin's boyfriend. "Strange question, Frank," I say, trying to sound casual. "Has Caitlin turned up for work yet, do you know?" He's on safe ground here and answers with confidence,

"No, no, she's not arrived yet and I would know, I'm always here as they open up. A bit late I'd say – for her, like," he adds. I can see him trying to readjust – he had us down as living together, thinking of the times I would turn up with Tomas to meet Caitlin from work at the end of the day. Now I can see he's not so sure.

"Could you ask her to give me a call when she gets here?" I consider waiting until nine-thirty – that way I can be certain that Caitlin is not in work – but I know it would be too weird for Frank. "It's Gregory," I add when I see the bemused look on his face.

I decide to act on the advice I gave Tomas and carry on as though this were a day like any other. Caitlin's workmates would find it pretty strange to see me waiting at the back door – plus, it would be the source for plenty of office gossip – so I leave. I walk around to the bakery and buy a fresh loaf, still warm and surely one of the finest things in this world? As I reach home the bread has me half-crazy with hunger. I make a coffee and enjoy the moment before settling down to work. What else is there to do?

I often listen to music as I sit down to work and more often than not then it's Bruce Springsteen. I love the way he tells a story, conjuring up a whole life in just five minutes and I guess I hope that some of his genius will rub off on me.

I sometimes think that the whole of what I want to achieve as a writer is in the song 'Point Blank'. There's one image in there – of the girl looking up, recognising Bruce and then turning away, refusing to acknowledge their shared past together – that is at the very heart of everything I try to write. Their relationship hasn't lived up to all she's hoped for and she's not interested in trying any more. Bruce of course, while accepting that things haven't quite worked out as planned, is still prepared to give it one last go.

He does the same with 'Stolen Car', when he sings about how he can't carry on living this way and trying to keep something alive long after it's gone. You don't need to have stolen a car to understand the song – I can't even drive a car, let alone steal one – but I remember from my own thieving days what it's like to have something you know can't possibly last. In these songs the past is a time of hope, when young lovers believe that what they share together can survive. Life may not be perfect but anything is better than giving up and letting the world win.

As I sit down to write I think how for years I've been trying to achieve a literary equivalent of Bruce's song/stories. I can pinpoint it to a specific time, soon after I started seeing Leta and I borrowed her brother's tape of *The River*. (Leta's brother's girl-friend's tape actually, and she'd recorded it in turn from her sister's record and no, I don't think Bruce is missing our money.) In fact, to this day the only copy I have of *The River* is another tape they recorded for me, edited to exclude what we considered to be the crap songs. I've listened to this tape again and again over the years – more than getting Leta's brother's girl-friend's sister's money's worth from Bruce. The only problem is the way it cuts out halfway through the last track, 'Wreck on the Highway'. Well not the only problem; the other one is that I'm not sure of the lyrics as I sing and play along on my imaginary guitar because I don't have the original sleeve notes.

Today I'm up and miming to 'Dancing in the Dark', adopting Bruce's stance from the video and standing in a part of the room not visible from the street. The music drowns out the idiocy of what I'm doing. I tell myself this is just a different form of dancing but deep down I know it; this really is stupid. Caitlin goes missing and I play air guitar – not the most grown-up of reactions, I guess. Unfortunately, the music can't drown out what's happened in the past week, specifically in the past eighteen hours. Trying to act normal and stick to my routine is one thing; acting like a prick at a time like this is quite another. I sit back down and try to get on with my work.

I had a school friend who would play the song 'Candy's Room' over and over again but only when I met Leta did I understand why. The deadly combination of falling in love and trying to be a writer had me hooked. So what if Bruce sang of places I knew nothing about? If I was looking for urban decay then where better than the Salford Docks? Manchester may not have a river worth talking about but what it does have is a Ship Canal full of shit and OK, nobody's going to dive in there as a symbol of hope and renewal, but they might drive up into the hills and swim in the reservoirs – that would work.

Most of my writing from back then was directly influenced by my Bruce obsession – I know, I know, another addiction – and I'm not saying I'm free of it yet. But to tell the story of a life, not a whole life but the essence of a life in such short, graphic images; surely this is no bad thing? It's the story! Without the story then you're fucked; tell it well and watch as everything else falls into place. Yes, I'm a sucker for 'Independence Day' and no, I'm not ashamed of using it to tell my own story. How else would I find a way to talk about the death of my father? How else to say that at the time I simply had to leave to get away; how, though I swore I'd never be like him, I find out now that we're more alike than ever. Tell me, how else should I say these things?

I hope that one day I can tell a story with an image as strong as these songs.

Mary, of Roger and Mary fame, is a staff nurse and I call her after lunch. I phone her at home because I know she's on nights and will be up around now. Also, I've avoided this for the whole morning – pretending to work, trying to act normal – because I feel so fucking stupid. My one attempt at anything practical hadn't gone too well when I rang Ann at Caitlin's workplace. Well, I say my one attempt; mid-morning I'd also phoned looking for Caitlin though I knew in my heart she wasn't there. I don't know what's wrong but I do know that whatever it is, Caitlin wouldn't carry on at work while not coming home.

"One moment," the receptionist said when I asked for Caitlin, and then, a few moments later –

"Who's this?" asked another – male – voice but the line went dead before I could answer.

So an hour later I'd phoned and asked for Ann. I was put straight through.

"Ann, Gregory."

"Gregory sorry, it's not a good time. I'll call you after work."

"Is she there?" I asked.

"What?"

"Is Caitlin in work?"

"No. Got to go."

Fucking great, I thought. Just about everybody else I know through Caitlin actually works with her. There are a couple of other friends I have in mind to call with Tomas this evening, as a way of appearing to be doing something, although to be honest I believe Caitlin will be back by then. I don't know why but I reckon for some reason she'll keep to working hours despite not being in work.

So it strikes me as a little early to be phoning the hospitals just yet. I'm hoping that phoning Mary will give me an idea of what the right thing to do might be. I'm that out of touch with what's considered normal.

"Mary, hi."

"Hi Greg, how's things?"

"I've not woken you have I?"

"No, no, I've been up an hour or so. How's life?" When we call each other it's generally because one couple or the other realise it's been over a month since we were in touch. A case of, do you think we should meet up with us being the best of friends and everything? "Are you thinking of coming over?" They live about ten miles away now on the other side of Manchester.

"Yeah, we should," I say vaguely and then "Mary?"

"Yes?"

"Has Caitlin contacted you at all, today or yesterday?"

"No, why? Unless she called Roger last night, but I think he would have said. We often have half-conversations while he's getting up and I'm going to bed. Is everything OK?"

"No," I say. "Caitlin didn't come in from work last night and she's not in work today."

"Then where is she, do you know? I guess not, otherwise why would you be calling?"

I describe to Mary my meeting with Caitlin yesterday lunchtime and how there's been nothing since.

"Are you worried? Sorry, silly question – of course, you are. Can you think of where she may have gone?"

"No. I called Ann last night, not because I thought she'd be there but because I thought Ann would know if anything had upset Caitlin during the day."

"And there was nothing?"

"No."

"And how's she been, I mean, since the hospital and everything?"

"Not good, as you can imagine, but I really thought she was pulling out of it."

"But now you think something's set her off again?"

"Something like that."

"But where would she go and why wouldn't she call?" A moment and then, "You don't think she may have had an accident do you?"

"I don't know," I say. "Given what she's been through in the past week or so, my bet is she needs time on her own. Maybe not calling is a part of that – it wouldn't count as time on her own if she called to let me know."

"Did you check the hospitals, the A. and E. departments?"

"No, that's why I'm calling you. Do you think I should?"

"Well, it would do no harm and at least it puts your mind at rest."

"You don't think it's too soon?"

"Not if she's had an accident, no."

"What do you do," I ask, "call each hospital?"

"No," says Mary, "there's a general number to call – I have it here somewhere. I'll give them a ring and then call you back."

"Would you?"

"Yes but it's most unlikely anything will come of it. She would have had some form of I.D. on her wouldn't she?"

"Yes, she even carries a donor card." How my mind is working.

"And are you the contact person on the card?"

"I believe so, yes."

"Then they'd already have called you. All they may be able to say is if they have an unidentified body that resembles Caitlin."

"Great," I say.

"Sorry," says Mary, "I'm still in work mode. I'll call you back in a few minutes."

She does so and confirms there's no report of anything that could possibly involve Caitlin.

"Call me this evening Greg, before nine. I'll have spoken to Roger by then and see if we can come up with any ideas. Maybe she'll be back by then?"

"Maybe," I agree.

"Look after yourself," she says and is gone. This is so crap – now our best friends know just how fucked up we really are.

Accidents – you're always close, just a few inches away. You don't have to travel in a car but it helps. There are no easy rules to follow here – if an accident's about to happen, there's nothing you can do to avoid it. It's in the very nature of the thing – why else would we call it an accident? An event that is without cause; an unforeseen course of events; an unintentional act, chance, misfortune – wow, I'll take any of those. Or maybe acts of nature are the only true accidents? It's hardly an unforeseen course of events when one car crashes into another. I guess there was a time when accidents weren't so associated with cars – maybe in the agricultural age, and certainly as the industrial age dreamt up new ways of killing people in the workplace. And all the while there's the spilt milk in the home, sharp knives and cupboard doors to walk into. There's really no saying what might happen out there.

Cars are where it's at for me though: there's nothing quite like that sound of metal hitting something at speed. They say a tree is the worst thing you can crash into, that a solid concrete wall has more give in it than a tree but whatever a car might hit, everybody knows that sound, so final and so certain.

As a child I stop playing to watch a car speed by, faster than I've ever seen a car travel in my life. It's the noise that catches my attention; first the revving of the engine, then the screeching of the tyres and then the moment's silence before I hear the grinding crush of metal into concrete. It's a textbook example and I see the whole thing; the car's crazy speed (probably nothing by today's standards), the distance it travels while braking (what, I think, cars don't just stop?) and then the flip into the air (ah, that silence – no engine, no brakes, no tyres – make it last, please, make it last) before the car lands with a crash, lodged on the concrete fencing by the side of the road.

The wreck of the car is suspended high above me on a collapsed concrete post, hanging there like a P.O.W. who's been shot climbing the perimeter fence. I trace the car's flight, back along the grass verge to where it first left the ground. I realise that this car must have a driver and surely he's dead? But then I see a crowd of people gathering some distance away by the side of the road. Hard as it is to imagine anything better than this wreck, I'm drawn away and see that the driver has survived. There he is, sat in amongst the crowd, drinking a cup of tea and shaking his head.

Adults usher us kids away but I've seen enough. What I want to know is, where did he get that cup of tea and how so quickly? I hear a phrase – thrown free – that I will hear time and again in my adult life; I can't imagine how a body can be thrown from a crashing car. What – a door just pops open or you're sucked through an open window? I hear the word lucky, I hear the word foolish and I hear the word playground. I have the feeling that while everybody's happy the driver's alive – several of the crowd make to pat him on the back just to get a touch, maybe to pick up on some of his luck – they also believe he had it coming, driving like a lunatic so close to where their children play.

And if it's your own child in the crash, how do you feel then?

I'm sat in the front passenger seat of my father's car. My brother is driving and Brenda is sat alone in the back. We're on our way home from a drinking party out in some woods with a group of friends who are following in the car behind. My brother has drunk too much to be driving; Brenda says as much before we set off but he's young and about to learn the hard way. It's a cold night and visibility is poor, both from the freezing fog outside and the warmth of our drunken breath on the windscreen. I wipe the window clear with a cloth for my brother before unfastening my seatbelt and climbing over into the back with Brenda.

What was I thinking, leaving her alone to sit in the back here? Brenda laughs her deep throaty laugh and we get down to some serious kissing. Brenda's laugh often confuses me; I think its part of her quick intelligence, that she sees the world in a different way. She chooses to laugh instead of what –? Is crying the only other option? But she stops laughing and we stop kissing when my brother leans across the dashboard to wipe the windscreen and steers the car off the road.

The road is little more than a dirt track that cuts a way through the woods. We're travelling slowly, say between 20 and 30mph. Once the front tyre leaves the track, my brother can't correct the direction of the car and the speed carries us through the wooden stakes that line the side of the road. These are huge six-inch square beams of wood designed to do this very job and, because they're not trees with roots deep into the ground, they give way sufficiently to slow down the car. They don't give way that easily though and the impact of each stake batters the nearside of the car into submission. I reckon we hit at least seven of them before the car comes to a stop, impaled high on the final stake. We know this because we can see the wood coming up through the floor of the car, lodged in the leg space of the front passenger seat. The whole front side of the car is compacted into where I'd been safely fastened in only moments before.

The three of us – Brenda, my brother and myself – remain in our seats and look at the wooden post.

So much for sitting in the front with your seat-belt fastened, I think.

It's difficult to make out anything else in the darkness of the woods until our friends in the car behind pull over and shine their headlights our way. Then, of course, we're blinded by the light but we gradually adjust and see enough to jump down from the car. I reach up to ease Brenda down and we take in the view, which is not good. All our luck has gone into saving our lives and it's obvious the car is a write off. The enormity of what he's done is beginning to hit my brother and he paces up and down along the side of the car.

"Fucking hell!" he says and shakes his head each time he stops to look at the car – so quick and simple how your world can change.

"At least you're safe," says someone, "that's the important thing."

Yes, we're safe, but what now? There's no way we can get away with this; no way of hiding the evidence or of covering up the facts – this car is crashed and staying crashed. We're drunk and, though we may be sobering up fast, it's obvious why this has happened. The others drive away to call my father and he decides to leave it till the morning and daylight before attempting to recover the car. The police aren't involved – what do they need to know about a car abandoned in the middle of some woods?

Somehow we all get home. Brenda stays over and this maybe eases things as we arrive. I can't help thinking though, over and over; this changes everything, this changes everything.

The next morning, before I'm even out of bed, the wreck is delivered to the house by a recovery truck. My heart sinks; I hate this car. The cars of our neighbours are all newer and smarter than ours. I hate the fact that we've moved to this neighbourhood if we can't hold our own – better to appear wealthy in a poor area than to appear poor in this one. And now the car is back, or at least most of the car, and it's more of an eyesore than ever. I go to find my brother.

"What's the car doing here?" I ask him.

He's been up since first thing and out with my father and the recovery guy to find where the car was crashed in the woods.

"The garage guy says the engine's more or less OK. It started first time when we tried it."

And sure enough, outside I hear the engine turning over. My brother goes to the door and shouts to ask my father if there's anything he can do to help. My father shakes his head, no. I look at my brother and think, what did he possibly believe he could do? I see my father sitting behind the wheel of the car, just sitting there, apparently doing nothing but listening, maybe, as the engine ticks over.

Everyone else – my mother Annie and brothers and sisters – are elsewhere, overshadowed by events. This is all about my brother and father. Not for me though – for me this is all about our crappy family and the life we lead. Brenda is there too; she gives me the excuse to get out the house and see her home.

As we walk past my father he continues staring into space and doesn't even reply when Brenda calls goodbye. I can see that although the wing of the car is compacted into the front passenger seat, the engine itself is untouched.

"I can't believe he's going to try to fix it," I say to Brenda, once we're clear of the house. However I feel about the car, it's nothing compared to what I think of my father's intention to rebuild it.

"What choice does he have?" she asks, but it's almost five years before I can see this.

The car stays in the driveway for weeks as piece-by-piece my father puts it back together again. He's unable to claim on the insurance because my brother was drunk and besides, this accident never officially happened. No panel beater is ever going to be able to fix the wing, so my father scours the local scrap yards for parts. First to be replaced are the main wheel rim and the bonnet so it at least starts to resemble the shape of a car again. But all of this costs money and it gets to be serious money for the headlights and the wrecked electrics; money to fix a car he could barely afford in the first place.

The longer this goes on, the greater my resentment and embarrassment. The problem is it's never going to look like a proper car again; it's never really going to look right. I'm exasperated that this thing is still in our driveway, so exasperated that I'm quickly getting over any lingering guilt I may have had about the night of the accident. I transfer my resentment from the car to my father: why does he have this obsession with rebuilding the car? Why can't he just use a garage like anyone else or sell it for the scrap it really is? I see him one day painting some form of a paste on to the wing of the car and it looks for a moment to be made from cardboard and glue.

I swear I'll never drive anything other than a brand new car.

After three months the car is roadworthy and my brother's asking to use it again. I tell him I think he's crazy, but then what do I know? His first time out, he inches gradually from a blind corner to check the oncoming traffic and a motorbike hits him, destroying the car for a second time. The driver of the motorbike is thrown free and suffers only minor injuries; my brother's unhurt. This time the police are called. The other guy agrees he's at fault and the insurance pay up. My father can buy – if not a brand new car, then at least a better car. My brother decides never to drive again; people try to persuade him but thankfully he holds out. He hopes to live his full and natural life.

Yes, it takes me almost five years to see my father had no choice but to rebuild his car. Five years to remember that in the days after the accident he never once added to my brother's guilt by shouting at him; he knew that, as a punishment, nothing could improve upon the fright my brother got from the crash. This thing was done, what else could he do? As he worked on the car he knew it looked like shit, though he would have never expressed it in those terms Money governed his every choice – the scrap value was nothing and he could barely afford replacement parts. So he did what he could.

And it takes me five years – in which time I move away from home, get on with my own life and start my own family – to realise that my father didn't just make do with the car; he did what was expected of him every day of his life. He was in it for the long haul. But by the time I understand what that means – what it takes to dig in for your family – it's too late: I only get it when my father is knocked off his pushbike and killed by a motorcyclist who is looking the wrong way.

You don't always need a car to have a good accident.

Four

Tomas may have been focussed on school all day but this ends the moment the bell rings. He rushes out the door, first to check that I'm there waiting and then to ask his big question.

"Has my Mum come home?"

He knows the answer when he sees my face. (Or how I guess my face looks. Foremost in my mind is concern for Tomas, and maybe I'm also a little angry with Caitlin, but often my face doesn't accurately reflect what I'm thinking.)

"No," I say, "she's not at home."

I can see he's thought this through and his reaction is one of determination; in the likely event that his Mum is still missing then he knows there are things we can be doing, steps we can be taking.

"Did she go to work?" He's checking up on me, making sure I've at least made some attempt to find her.

"No," I say. "I phoned twice and the second time I spoke to Ann – your Mum's not there."

We walk past Caitlin's workplace as we make our way home and he looks across at the building, thinking God knows what.

"And she didn't call? There's no message?"

"No, son, there was no message."

"Maybe she'll be there when we get home?"

He's being plucky so I don't dishearten him. I believe Caitlin will come home this evening, with an explanation – a justification – that I may have issues with but one I'll be able to live with when all is said and done. Taking one day out is not so bad after all and the time may come in the future when I need to do the same.

What I'm not looking forward to is phoning around this evening if Caitlin doesn't appear but as we make our way home,

Tomas is already talking about who best to call. I dismiss a few of them because they're workmates of Caitlin and I persuade Tomas that we have that covered with Ann. Although, if I'm honest, I know that if Caitlin is staying with a work friend and wants to keep it quiet then there's every chance she may not have told Ann. Also – and this only occurs to me as we walk – most of Caitlin's work friends are male; I don't want to think what this might mean.

"I called Mary this afternoon too," I say.

I can see the conflicting reaction in Tomas' eyes – pleased that I've been doing something but disappointed as another simple explanation for his mother's whereabouts is crossed off the list.

No, if Caitlin doesn't come back then the people we have to call this evening are the true friends she knew before I met her; the friends she made when she was alone, when she came back to Manchester and when Tomas was born. The friends I had hoped Caitlin needed less and less as she made her life with me.

First though, there's Suzie waiting to talk to us when we arrive home. It makes sense to ask her if she's heard anything – she is, after all, the source of all local knowledge – but I wouldn't normally choose to discuss something as private as this. It just seems to happen, in the same way that we know about John and Sarah upstairs; we all live too close for things not to come out.

"What's that girlfriend of yours been up to then?" she calls across the fence as I put the key in the door.

"What do you mean?" I ask, possibly a little too defensively. How could she know that Caitlin hadn't come home?

"Yes," says Tomas, boldly because it's Suzie, "what do you mean?"

Sometimes I suspect that Suzie spends most of her time in the front garden, even in the middle of winter, only to keep up with what's happening in the world – just as I shut myself up indoors, away from that world. There's always a good reason for her to be outside – gardening, painting – and somehow it doesn't come across as nosiness, more as an integral part of the neighbourhood.

"You haven't heard then?" she asks. This in the sure knowledge that I never know shit about what's going on.

A young woman, stunningly good-looking, comes out from Suzie's house.

"I'm going then," she says and kisses Suzie on the cheek.

"Uh-huh," says Suzie, playing it hard." We all watch the woman as she leaves through the gate.

"Jesus, Suzie," I say. "How do you do it?"

"You like that, do you?" She's trying to embarrass me in front of Tomas. "I'm not sure she'd be so interested in you."

"I don't doubt it for a second," I say. Suzie has a steady stream of young lovers. What fascinates me is not her sexuality but the time she keeps – this is Suzie just getting up while Tomas here has already finished his day at school.

"What do you mean about Caitlin?" I ask again.

"The fighting down at the Social – all hell was let loose down there today." I obviously don't know what she's talking about. Suzie may get up eight hours later than I do but she still finds out what goes on while she sleeps. "The knackers from number five went in and wrecked the place. The police were called and they had to close for the day. Caitlin hasn't called to tell you, no?"

There are so many things I don't understand here that I'm at a loss as to what to say. I sense Tomas is itching to ask about Caitlin, so I get in first.

"Number five?" I ask.

"You know, the house fire?"

"On the corner there?" The burnt-out house is number five on the estate.

"Yes, it sounds like we had a lucky escape there. A houseful of Irish knackers on the street, that's the last thing we need around here. Fucking hundreds of them," she says. "Whoever burnt them out did us all a huge favour."

"Knackers?" I say.

"You know," she says, "Irish scum. Begging your pardon

but they're not all like Caitlin, you know."

"And you reckon they were burnt out?" I ask. "Before they'd even moved in?"

"Well, it's a bit of a coincidence, isn't it?"

"But why would anyone want to do that?"

"It's a bit extreme, I agree," says Suzie laughing, "but I can't say I'm too upset. If today was anything to go by then I think they were a nasty bunch and good riddance to them is what I say."

"But what did they do? What happened?"

"They went down there this morning, took all their relatives too from the sound of it, and just went crazy. They smashed in the protective glass and attacked all the staff. That's when the police came."

Caitlin works on the public counter – for a second I picture her being attacked, but then I remember she wasn't even there. I know Tomas is dying to tell Suzie that his Mum wasn't in work.

"Was anyone hurt?" I ask.

"They got one guy quite badly; anyone else was just caught by the glass when they rammed it through with a table." She laughs again. "I think they were hell-bent on wrecking the place and from what I can make out it sounds as though they made quite a job of it. The place has been closed all day."

Now I understand why Ann couldn't talk when I called this morning.

"Hasn't Caitlin called to tell you all this?" Suzie's amazed – it would be the first thing she'd want to be told if her partner worked in the Social Security office. Again, I try to keep Suzie off the subject of Caitlin.

"What happened to the –" I don't know what to call them – "the family?"

"Family? Hah!" says Suzie. "They're not a family; they're just a bunch of Irish come over here pretending to be a family so they can get a house from the Social. I tell you, there were fifteen of them about to move in to that house – can you imagine the state of the place? And that's nothing compared to how many more would follow. Once they set up camp somewhere they use it to bring all sorts of characters over and before you know it, we're overrun with them. No, it may sound a bit harsh Gregory but we're well rid of them. They were a bad lot."

"But I mean, what happened to them after the fire? Were they inside when it happened?" I'm trying to think back to Sunday night but it seems this was a very quiet fire.

"No," says Suzie. "They were due to move in yesterday. Whoever set the place on fire aren't barbarians – they just wanted to send a message, that's all."

"So they probably went in to the Social on Monday?"

"I suppose – they must have expected to move in and then when they saw what had happened…"

Then they went straight to the Social and probably straight to Caitlin – a nice case to come across on your first day back at work. Tomas can stand it no longer.

"My Mum wasn't in work today," he tells Suzie.

"Was she not, darling? Then she was well out from what I can make out. Is she still off sick?" she asks me.

It would be very easy to give Suzie this line but again Tomas has to tell all.

"We don't know where she is," he says.

"What do you mean, my love? You don't know where your Mum is?"

"She's gone missing," says Tomas.

"Well," I say, "we don't know" but there's no stopping Tomas.

"She didn't come home last night and she didn't go in to work today," he informs Suzie. She looks up at me.

"We're guessing she had a bad day yesterday and then went out last night. That's why I was asking when that family were in the Social – if Caitlin was given that case on her first day back then, I don't know," I finish lamely.

"But she hasn't called?" asks Suzie.

"No," Tomas and I answer together.

Suzie knows immediately that this is too odd, that

something is definitely not right here, but in front of Tomas she lets it pass.

"Maybe she's still recovering from her hangover?" she says.

"That's more or less what we were thinking," I reply. "We'll just have to wait and ask her this evening." I want it to seem to Suzie as though the Caitlin thing is no big deal. I open the door and try to usher Tomas inside before he says anything else.

"Are you coming in with me for a while?" Suzie asks Tomas.

I let him choose and of course he stays with Suzie. I know she'll quiz me later if Caitlin fails to turn up – more out of concern than nosiness, I think – and she's sure to pick stuff up from Tomas, but what can I do? Suzie allows Tomas to talk away at her; I'm not too sure how much she listens but I know it's this that he loves about her.

The days may be bright but as the sun disappears then you know soon enough that winter's still here and there's a while to go before spring. It's dark and cold outside and not much better inside. My feeble attempt at making a fire barely has any effect on the living room, let alone on the rest of the flat. We have to resort to wood fires at the moment – we refuse to burn scab coal – and they just don't give out the same heat. We're the only ones amongst all our friends who are dependent on an open fire and the back yard is full of cuttings and branches they've brought round to see us through the miners' strike. Roger brought half a tree on his last visit but I've yet to attack it with my saw. As we were carrying it through the garden, I slipped and the huge trunk landed between my legs, missing my balls by an inch.

"That was close," said Roger.

"Too close. How about warning me next time there's a step?"

I sat on my arse, straddling the tree and laughing nervously with relief.

"That would have hurt," said Roger.

"It would have settled one thing, though."

"What's that?"

"Whether we can have children or not."

"It's a painful way to find out."

"Is there any easy way? Come on, let's move it over here – and carefully this time."

There seems to be little point in building up a fire tonight – not if, as I suspect, Tomas and I will soon be in bed. I'm torn between this practicality and the make-believe of a warm house for Caitlin to come home to but I'm not having another night like last night, no way.

Ann calls immediately after six, probably waiting first for the cheap rate to kick in. She doesn't stand on ceremony.

"What the hell was Caitlin thinking?" she asks.

I ask Tomas to turn the telly down a little.

"Thinking about what?" I ask. I like Ann but sometimes she can rub you up the wrong way.

"Can I speak to her?"

"She's not here, Ann."

"She's not there?"

"No," I say.

"What, she still hasn't come home?"

"No."

"Then what's she doing? What's she playing at?"

"If I knew that Ann…"

"Yes, of course, but – oh, I don't know, she can be her own worst enemy sometimes."

Well, I think, this is a good start to the evening's phone calls.

"What happened at work today?" I ask.

"You heard then?" says Ann without actually telling me anything. "I don't know what Caitlin thought she was doing on Monday evening but she created a right mess. Can you imagine the chaos? This changes everything – the way the office is run, how we deal the public – everything. Any sympathy we may have had for that family, or any harsh cases in the future, it will all be very different from now on."

I'm not interested in where this is going – if Ann can't tell me where to find Caitlin then I don't want to listen to tales from the workplace.

"And you think Caitlin had something to do with what happened today?"

"Well, what do you think?" she says. "That's what Caitlin was working on when she was last in work. All her case notes are missing and now you tell me that Caitlin's missing too. Where was she this morning when those bastards came back? Maybe then she'd have seen what she started."

I don't know what Ann is saying here – well, I do know but I don't know how much of it she believes. It would be understanding of me to put Ann's attitude down to a bad day at the office but I don't feel much like being understanding.

"The police want to speak to her," she continues.

"The police – why?"

"Why do you think Gregory? Because she was the one working on the case."

"Ann, you don't really believe that Caitlin was responsible for what happened today?" The idea of Caitlin starting a riot, or even encouraging a riot, is ridiculous. I don't give Ann a chance to reply. "Do you know where Caitlin is?" I ask.

"No," she says.

"And nobody at work has heard anything from her?"

"Not to my knowledge and anyway, I think they'd have told the police."

"The police were at the Social?"

"Yes, it was that bad."

"And they were looking for Caitlin?"

"What else do they have to go on? You have to admit it's strange that she's gone missing?"

"Yes, but not for that reason."

"I wouldn't be surprised if they call on you," says Ann.

"What – here?"

"Well, they think she took today off sick but if she doesn't turn up tomorrow then they're going to wonder where she could be."

"Aren't we all?" I say. "Let me know if you hear anything, would you?"

Tomas is eager to do the phone-around but if this is any

indication of how the evening will go, then I'm not so keen. I make myself something to eat, not bothering with the pretence of a proper meal for the family. As I do so, I suggest to Tomas he gets ready for bed.

"But what about the phone calls?" he says and I know I can't avoid them.

"You get ready for bed and then we'll call," I say.

I start with an easy one by calling Mary's number again and speak to Roger.

"Still no sign of her?" he asks and I go over the few things I know. I tell him about the trouble at the Social and also about the house being burnt out down the road.

"Something like that would seriously upset her," I say, "especially if she realised they were going to be living close by."

"She takes it all so personally," says Roger. "I don't know whether she's suited to be on that front counter."

This is rich coming from Roger who has to cope with Mary each time a patient dies. Both our partners have difficult jobs but you couldn't picture either of them doing anything else for a living.

"But Caitlin's good at it," I say. "Can you imagine how some of those other fuckers in there would cope? You're right though – she couldn't help but take it to heart."

We chat for a while but I can see Tomas is becoming impatient – this isn't getting us anywhere.

"Irish girls, eh?" says Roger.

"Tell me about it," I agree. "I'll call you tomorrow, or sooner if I hear anything."

"We have to phone Rosie and Bill," says Tomas as soon as I put down the phone.

"I know, son." And I do know; I just don't want to do it. These are Caitlin's friends, not mine. They have a history together that I don't share – I'm just a Johnny-come-lately to these people and I don't want to involve them in our affairs.

"I'll dial the number," says Tomas and he does so. I doubt if I have a record of their number in the house – it would be kept in Caitlin's address book – but Tomas knows it by heart. He hands the receiver to me.

"Hi Bill, it's Gregory."

"Oh hi," he says. "How are you?"

"Fine, thanks." I like Bill but it's Rosie I have to speak to and I ask to speak to her.

"Gregory," she says as she picks up the phone from Bill. "What can I do for you?"

I've never once phoned Rosie or Bill before tonight; we've met and we get along fine and they are absolutely OK by me but we all know it's strange that I should be calling.

"Rosie, Caitlin didn't come home last night and she wasn't in work today. I don't know where she is and I'm worried."

"Well, I…"

This pause is the reason I didn't want to call. It means that Rosie knew this day would come; that Caitlin may have moved away but it was only a matter of time before Rosie took this call. This pause means that Rosie and Bill were there for Caitlin when she needed them once before and they'll be there for Caitlin when she needs them again. It means that I may think I'm here to stay but that Rosie thinks otherwise. I may believe I have what it takes but let's just wait and see. It means I might think I know Caitlin but Rosie knows her better than I do. And what Rosie knows is that Caitlin will always choose her partners badly; I may have seemed to be the exception but now the moment's here then Rosie's hardly surprised.

Or maybe I have her wrong, I don't know.

"She hasn't come home this evening?" Rosie asks.

"No."

"And no phone call – nothing?"

"Well, that's why I'm phoning; to see if she's been in touch with you."

"No, Gregory, I'm sorry."

We go through the usual things. Is it the results from the hospital – Caitlin wasn't shy in letting all her friends know – maybe she went back to work too soon; have I checked with the hospitals and who else have I called?

I don't know, these are good people but I just have the feeling they've been waiting for this to happen, or at least if not this then something else along these lines. Yes, they're concerned, particularly for Tomas, but I get the feeling they think Caitlin is more than capable of looking after herself.

What am I saying here? Come on Gregory – spit it out! OK, this is it – I think they believe I must have done something to Caitlin for her to leave Tomas and disappear, even if only she's only been gone for a day and one night.

Of course, no such thing is said and of course they'll phone if she gets in touch but I get little else out of them.

Tomas forces me to repeat the exercise with another of Caitlin's friends. I avoid any further calls by asking this last person to phone around their network of friends. Sure, let them all talk but it's our best chance of getting a message to Caitlin; that is, so long as Caitlin wants to be found.

This also seems to satisfy Tomas for the evening. I suggest he sleeps with me in my bed; he's probably as keen as I am to avoid the horrors of last night and the novelty might help him settle. I tuck him into the double bed. I hug him and kiss him but I can't pretend to know just how bad he must be feeling. Even this, sleeping in his mother's bed, is a tacit admission that she's unlikely to come home tonight. I can't promise him everything will be OK because I'm not sure it will. Yet if Tomas is feeling bad, he doesn't show it. He looks unhappy sure, but not distraught and he seems to accept my assurances that whatever his Mum may be doing, we have to trust that she knows what's best. This is as much as I can do for him – what else is to be said to a five year old boy whose mother's not come home?

"Are you going to phone Grandma Annie?" he asks as he settles into the bed.

"No, why? Do you think I should?"

The thought of calling my mother and starting to explain all this over the phone doesn't appeal; plus, I can't see any immediate benefit from doing so.

"That's what I'd do," says Tomas. "She would know what to do."

He pushes himself up on to his elbow to talk but I don't encourage him.

"Come on," I say, "we've had enough phone calls for one night."

His eagerness to call my mother has more to do with seeing me keep in closer touch than with the whereabouts of his own. I pull the bedclothes up around his shoulders and he lies back down. I can see he's all in and will be asleep in no time. I kiss him on his forehead.

"Are you coming to bed soon?" he asks quietly.

"Give me five minutes," I say but Tomas is so tired I doubt he even hears my reply. I know there's a danger that if I go to bed too soon, I may wake up in the middle of the night but I'm prepared to take the chance. However reassuring it is for Tomas to be sleeping in our bed, I'm hoping he has as calming an effect on me.

There's one final strange event on this, my first day as a single parent. I'm brushing my teeth in the bathroom when there's a knock at the front door and my heart sinks. I really don't want to see anyone tonight – not that I ever do anyway – and the thought of talking to anyone doesn't appeal in the slightest.

We have a sign in the hallway that reads *Céad Míle Fáilte* but its Caitlin's sign and her philosophy, not mine. A hundred thousand welcomes – I don't think so. I'm not the most welcoming person in the world, as Caitlin discovered one evening when a local nun came calling to the door. I opened the door and this nun tried to dodge past me into the house. I couldn't believe it: she presumed she had an automatic right of entry to my home, just because she was a nun? I blocked the doorway and as she went one way then I blocked again as she tried to dodge past me. From the back, of course, all Caitlin could see was Gregory being rude to a visitor –again – and in the end I had to concede. Caitlin paid the price though, when she realised it was just another nun looking for money.

I don't like unexpected callers. In my experience they rarely bring good news and never arrive at the right time. The knock on the door is likely to disturb Tomas just as I have him settled; I'm reconciled to another night without Caitlin; and I really feel as though it's the end of my day. Yes, it's early, but what's that to the world? Why should I care what other people make of me? I'm tempted to pretend I'm not here, to ignore the knock at the door, but the lights are a giveaway and if they knock again they'll wake Tomas.

I think of Ann saying that the police might well call for Caitlin. I even consider for a moment that it may be Caitlin, knocking on her own front door. But then I realise it's probably Suzie, reckoning on Tomas being in bed and hoping to finish our conversation from this afternoon. Each time I talk to someone though, the fact that Caitlin's missing becomes less and less real; the more I repeat what I know and don't know, the more removed I am from how I really feel. If I had a choice, I would keep it all to myself; perhaps I'd ring Roger and Mary but that would be all. Anyone else is just for Tomas' sake, to let him feel we're doing something. Talking to other people doesn't make things any better for me; it just makes them stranger. Now Suzie's here and I guess I have to go through it one more time – yes, Caitlin was upset; yes, we've had some bad news; yes, I think she went back to work too soon; and no, I don't think that was an ideal first day back. (Nobody's mentioned John beating the shit out of Sarah yet; I don't think they realise that it's likely to be this more than anything that would keep Caitlin away from home.)

"Oh," I say as I answer the door. It's Olivia, Suzie's daughter.

"Hi," she says. "Mum wants to know if you need anything?"

"No," I say. "Thanks. Tell Suzie thanks."

"Is Caitlin back?"

"No, there's still no sign of her." This is the point where I should invite Olivia in, or rather, where anybody else would invite her in.

"Do you think she's OK?"

"I hope so. I think she's just had enough and needs a break for a few days. You know, with work and everything?"

Olivia nods as though she understands but doesn't say

anything or move to go. She stands there, cold in the night air. She's not dressed for the cold, as though she's expecting to be asked in.

"Was Suzie worried?" I ask, if only for something to say.

"Yes, well, we both were," she says and again stands silent for a moment. Then she says, "I just thought I'd call to see if you needed anything." She looks me full in the face as she says this but then almost immediately looks back down at the ground. "I mean, if you wanted to go out for a drink or something, I could mind Tomas for you."

"No, thanks, I'm fine," I say. "That's very kind of you – and would you say thanks to Suzie for me?"

Olivia nods again but still doesn't move. What does she want?

"Well," I say, "thanks," and I close the door.

Was that really what I think it was? I can't believe it – it's not as though it's never occurred to me; how could it not with a girl like Olivia next door? It's just that, well, I'm surprised. She's beautiful but she's young. And she chooses today of all days to let me know? Or perhaps she's heard that Caitlin may have left? Talk about a fast mover – I wonder did Suzie encourage her to call round?

I shake my head; this is too much for one day. I lock the door and put the chain across the latch. I get undressed and climb into bed with Tomas. I sleep through the night and Caitlin doesn't come home.

As Imran takes her case it's obvious to Caitlin that she's being allowed back in. She finds she can't look at him directly but looks instead to one side, into the hallway light. She can feel the warmth as it escapes the house into the night air, can actually feel the movement of the air as it brushes past her face. She has taken off her dark glasses but is still wearing her headscarf. She hopes that Imran will approve of her covered head, that it will say something to him that she doesn't know how to put into words. She bows her head.

Imran takes her hand, the hand that had been holding the

case, and guides her into the hall. Still, he doesn't say a word but this gentle act of kindness tells Caitlin she's forgiven. Imran closes the door, shutting out the cold behind them. The hallway is large and long; the whole house is large and long and, despite being old with high ceilings, is always kept warm and bright in winter, cool and dark in summer. Any draughts that can be prevented have long been banished and those that remain are blasted with heat and extra carpeting. Rugs take the edge off the hardwood floor, and heavy curtains shut away the large bay windows to create a cocoon of warmth and comfort. Throws cover the furniture and hangings cover the large expanses of wall.

Imran works with his two brothers importing textiles, while also becoming increasingly preoccupied with running his own separate business – mainly in response to an idea of Caitlin's. Soon after they moved to Leeds she showed Imran what he was taking for granted – that the quality of product he could bring over from Pakistan was far superior to anything available in England. She told him that his instinct to always undercut on price wasn't necessarily right and she persuaded him to sell the rugs as a premium product, citing herself as the type of person who would willingly pay more for better quality.

At the time, Imran and his two brothers were doing most of their business trading in the markets, operating in various places at once. Although they were successful enough, Imran soon persuaded them to apply the same sales strategy as he had introduced to the textiles they were bringing in. While keeping the market stalls going, the brothers set themselves up as importers of fine goods and waited for other traders to come to them. England was changing and again it was Caitlin who pointed out the possibility of selling the same material to different customers at different prices. She took Imran to junk and antique stores, pointing to pottery imported from the Far East and, more importantly, to the prices they were charging. The one constant they had was the quality of goods they brought over; it was the choice of where they sold these goods that could make them all a lot of money.

Imran places the suitcase on the floor at the foot of the stairs and then helps Caitlin off with her coat. She unties the headscarf and hands it to him.

"Go through and make yourself warm," he says. "The fire is lit in the front room." They only use the coal fire on evenings such as these, when the central heating may do the hard work but the fire creates the real warmth, the warmth that matters.

"I'll take your things upstairs," he says and as he does so Caitlin wanders through into the front room, almost in a daze, and the tiredness of relief hits her. The few encouraging words from Imran are a thankful return to the ordinary. What's gone before, both last night and this afternoon, isn't to be forgotten or ignored but set to one side. There's blame and hurt on both sides and yet what is there to say about it? For her part, Caitlin is so beyond thinking that whatever may happen is all that can happen; she's too tired to fight, too tired to care any more.

Imran must feel the same – Caitlin could sense the sympathy as he opened the front door – and surely this says something for their life together? What ever else they may be, they are after all husband and wife, a unit and a team. Without each other then they're nothing. Caitlin can hear Imran moving around upstairs, presumably putting her clothes away and returning her belongings to their rightful place.

She closes her eyes. She knows she can never leave. This is her home and Imran is her husband. How can she leave when this and this alone is her life? If Caitlin's learnt one thing today then it's this fact, that there's no life for her other than here.

Imran is kneeling at Caitlin's feet, holding her hand. She must have fallen asleep.

"Caitlin?" He rubs the back of her hand, gently stroking her awake. She turns her hand over and holds on to Imran. She smiles and closes her eyes again.

"Caitlin? Have you eaten?"

"Mmm?"

"I haven't cooked anything. I was thinking we could go down the road and maybe eat out?"

"When did you ever cook anything?" asks Caitlin smiling,

still with her eyes closed. She squeezes his hand again, just to let him know she's winding him up. She knows he's trying his best, lighting the fire, and doing what he can to make this OK. "Maybe you're too tired?" says Imran. "I could order some food in if you prefer?"

Caitlin is happy just sitting here; she wants nothing more than to go to bed for the night and to sleep through until the morning. It seems so appealing but she fights the tiredness that is pulling at her because she knows it's unfair – Imran hates takeaway meals and his suggestion of a restaurant is an attempt at compromise.

"No," she says, "I'm fine. Let's just stay local though, shall we?"

"Are you sure that's OK?"

The last thing Caitlin wants is to go out again but the gratitude she feels and the love and the relief are even stronger than her tiredness.

"Pull me up," she says. She's recently taken to rolling out the armchairs; such is her shape and size. Before he helps her up, Imran places the palm of his hand gently on Caitlin's tummy.

"How's my little boy?" he asks.

"Kicking to get out," says Caitlin.

"I'm so proud of him already. I want him to have everything. I want everything to be right for him."

"If he has two people who love him then that's as much as anyone needs." Caitlin says this and means it but she's been the more insistent that everything should be right for when their baby arrives.

She had a difficult early pregnancy and, having miscarried the year before, there wasn't much she could do but sit at home and wait. She didn't dare hope, not wanting to tempt fate a second time, but once it looked as though this baby was safe, then she threw herself into getting the house prepared. She had so much time and no shortage of money, but then, she had no shortage of dreams either.

It was so devastating when their first baby had died. In retrospect she'd been so young, though it was only last year.

Everything had happened so quickly – falling in love, leaving home, getting married and moving away to Leeds – that when she became pregnant it just seemed natural that this should happen next. When the baby died inside her at five months, only then did Caitlin realise just how desperately important being pregnant had become. Only then did she realise that this was the whole purpose of her being. She wanted to have a family, to be a mother – the creator of and the carer for her children. She wanted to do this with the man she loved in this beautiful home. She wanted to replace and improve upon the broken version of a family she'd left behind. One day she might want for something more, something different, but – having learnt this about herself and been given the second chance– she could think of no finer hope than to fulfil this simple human need.

"Yes, I'd love to go out for a meal," she says to Imran. "Give me a few minutes to get ready."

She climbs the stairs slowly and, looking around the bedroom, sees that Imran has indeed put away her clothes. Is this the kind act of a guilty man or more a statement of intent? She walks along to the bathroom. The mirror tells a sorry story – her day's adventure has taken a heavy toll but she does what she can to freshen up. She lightly applies some make-up over her bruising but it's still too tender to do anything more than a gentle powder; besides, she's reluctant to deny completely what happened here. Returning to the bedroom, she considers changing her clothes but decides against it, given the limited options of what she can wear.

As she walks slowly down the stairs, there's a momentary registering of disappointment on Imran's face but he conceals it well. After all, this isn't really a full evening out together; they're just popping out to grab a bite to eat. They drive the short distance to the restaurant and Imran repeatedly checks that Caitlin is warm enough. He helps her in and out the car, taking her arm into the restaurant and holding her chair as she sits down. None of it seems overdone to Caitlin and anything is preferable to an anguished apology. She knows he's sorry, as she hopes he knows she's sorry, and this politeness is as good a platform as any to build upon.

She's worried when, after placing their orders, he takes her hand and is about to speak. She dreads talking about what's happened and fears that if she starts crying then she won't be able to stop. She tries to keep the conversation away from anything that may upset her.

"How did you get on today – did that shipment arrive OK?"

"Yes, yes, it was fine," says Imran. He rarely talks to Caitlin about his business and seems impatient whenever she tries, as though he doesn't like to be reminded just how much he owes to Caitlin.

"I want to say something," he says.

Oh no, no, no, no, no, thinks Caitlin. She wants desperately to avoid talking about the past twenty-four hours – this is why she's agreed to come to a public place – but she can see that Imran is determined.

"I know how important this baby is to you," he says, "and it is to me too, but I know just how much you want everything to be right."

Please, no, thinks Caitlin.

"And I also know I haven't been there enough for you these past few months – "

"You've been busy through work," says Caitlin. "Where would we be without all the money you bring in?"

"But still," says Imran, "I don't always have to be the one doing all the travelling and the late nights and the last minute calls to say I can't make it home."

"It's OK, I understand."

"I know you understand and you have been – very understanding, but from now on I want to be at home more and at work less. The others can cope without me and..." Imran pauses. "Although they're my brothers, I want you to know that this is my family now, we three people here."

"Oh Immy," says Caitlin. The tears are falling for a different reason, a happier one maybe, but still they're tears.

"I know how upset you were when we lost our baby last year – "

"Please Immy, don't! I can't, I know what you're trying to say and I know you mean well but not here. I can't, not here, not without making a show of myself." Caitlin stifles a laugh to show how silly she feels. "Let's just enjoy this evening and the food and us being together."

"I love you so much," says Imran.

"I know you do. Really. I know you do."

Five

On Wednesday morning, Tomas and I wake up to the fact that this is pretty much how things will be until Caitlin comes home. We don't talk much as we get ready, nor as we leave and walk to school. I make no pretence of coping well and I'm simply going through the motions. Tomas is just as bad; he doesn't want to go to school and is deliberately slow, refusing to increase his pace as he dawdles along behind me.

"Look," I stop and say at one point, "I'm not enjoying this either you know."

I walk on, feeling bad and angry now with myself for shouting at him. He deserves better than this; I'm just waiting to be free of him so I can get back home and into bed.

We make our peace at the school gates.

"I'm sorry for going so slow," he says.

"No, I'm sorry for losing my temper. We're not late, so don't worry."

The last few children are going into school and Tomas runs across the playground to join them. Once he's in the door, I walk over to Caitlin's workplace, thinking I can check in again with Frank the security guard but he's not there. There are two policemen guarding the staff entrance, presumably to prevent any repeat of yesterday's violence. I walk on through the car park as though I'm taking a short cut and I don't look back for fear of attracting attention to myself. The impression I get is of things having changed around here; I think they've been given quite a shock. However bad it was here yesterday though, it was nothing more than Caitlin has warned them about for months. Staff safety, proper security; these are not new issues – even I know that.

As I leave the car park I pass two of Caitlin's workmates on their way into the office.

"Hi, Gregory," they say together and then, "Is Caitlin OK? Will she be back in today?"

I tell them Caitlin's still sick and they don't seem surprised. Ann must have given the office this line yesterday and I'm grateful to her for this, if for nothing else.

"That was a terrible thing yesterday," says one of Caitlin's workmates. I know that if I stop to chat then she'll probably fill me in on the whole story but I just nod in agreement and walk on. I doubt if they can tell me anything to help figure out where Caitlin might be or what she's doing.

The stupid bitches are still going into work. They're precisely the types to jump to conclusions about Caitlin; I can imagine they were only too pleased to talk to the police yesterday. I don't know what happened – or what it had to do with Caitlin – but I do know that, once again, her workplace has impinged upon our home life. Whatever this was, it was more than just a bad day at the office. I think of all the support and encouragement I give Caitlin and realise it could never be enough for what she has to face out here in the world; this shit was always coming our way.

So I make my way home. There's no need to go to the baker's today. Once I'm home, I drink my coffee and eat some toast before getting back into bed.

I mean, what's the point? Caitlin's obviously doing whatever it is she wants to do, needs to do, and there's little or nothing I can do about it. Let's face it, Caitlin can do as she likes here and that includes going off with someone else. I keep telling myself it's unlikely but that doesn't stop it being a possibility. There's nothing about me that can't be replaced; it wouldn't be for the first time and it's probably not the last. Picture this: a man goes up to a complete stranger in a bar and tells her he'd like to sleep with her. Now picture this: a woman goes up to a complete stranger and tells him she'd like to sleep with him. Different rules, different results.

I don't know what Caitlin is doing; I don't know what she's thinking. For all her fear of me leaving her, she's the one that's gone missing. I don't know if she's hurting or if she's intent on hurting me. I don't know where she could be or who if anyone she may be with. I don't know what I should do in this situation – should I be phoning around continuously, running around desperately to feel as though I'm at least doing something? Whatever – I don't know what to do so I just go back to bed.

But even this gives me little or no comfort. It's so long since I felt close to Caitlin and I feel her absence even more in bed. At least when Tomas is with me then I don't feel so alone. The last bit of sexual activity I can recall is my trip alone to the hospital.

There's a sign on the door that tells me 'Strictly No Admittance Unless Authorised' but I have my appointment card so I walk on in. What's so special that it must be kept a secret from the general public? This is a casualty ward with a difference – no Accident and Emergency chaos; no blood, panic or shouting; no trolleys in the corridor. It's so perfectly quiet that I think I may have come to the wrong place. It's more like a research lab than a hospital but I see a bell to ring and after a few preliminary questions here I am, alone in a room with a glass test-tube in my hand. I have to laugh – I'm not too sure how to go about this and it's not the kind of occasion you'd ask for advice. There's nothing else to do but to drop my trousers and get on with it.

I look at the glass test-tube in my hand and think Christ, what if I come all over the floor? I'll have to keep my wits about me to avoid going through this a second time. Despite the best efforts of the nurse to put me at my ease, it's embarrassing for the two of us as she leaves me alone in the room. She suggests I leave my package on a table in the corridor; this will avoid any further awkwardness. I look around to see if she's left me any magazines but it looks as though this is where the Health Service draws the line. And then there are the surroundings – not exactly conducive, if you know what I mean. Everything is so clinically clean, with the washbasin and towel at the side just waiting for me to get on with it and be finished.

I think of Caitlin but this has nothing to do with her – it's hard to fantasize about someone you think you know so well. No, this is about wanting something you just can't have; it's about stealing something that isn't yours to steal. Of course this ward is out of bounds; here you can let your mind go free – just don't confuse it with everyday life. Enjoy your wank but don't think for one moment it's going to change a thing. So you'll forgive me if I don't tell you who or what I think about; let's just say I concentrate on my aim and it's a success. I pull up my trousers, wash my hands and replace the rubber top in the glass tube. If only sex was so simple.

I leave my sample on the table in the corridor, a freshly made bomb just waiting to explode.

So you see, that hardly qualifies as intimacy. I think of Olivia calling last night – is that what she was offering? Who's to say what might have happened if only I'd asked her in? I curse myself for being so fucking stupid at the time.

And, Caitlin? I look up at her suitcase on top of the wardrobe and I think it means she'll come home, but it's not a whole lot to go on. I just wish I knew where she was. I'm worried, and I'm angry too, because I told myself I'd never go through this again, not for anybody. Yet here I am, alone in my bed, not knowing where my partner may be or if she's ever coming home.

I don't know – if Caitlin wants to drive me back to Leta, if only to prove herself right, then she's going the right way about it.

I'm in bed with Leta; her body nestled into mine like some perfect fit, my arm around her shoulder with my hand resting on her upper arm. This is such a writer's room – a bed, a desk, a chair, a typewriter and a stereo – I'm so happy here. (Mind you, this attic room isn't so appealing after a while, typewriter or no typewriter, not when Leta starts to ask how I'm ever going to earn any money. She wants her partner to look after her, she doesn't want to work all her life, she wants to have children and start a family but we never get as far as trying.)

There's never a moment when I'm not acutely conscious of just how beautiful she is, never a time when I can't believe my luck because really, the times we're together are so few. Her leg is across mine so I can feel the heat from between her legs on my thigh. We're listening to Bruce drone on about driving all night to buy some shoes (why shoes – I have no idea) when Leta jumps up, demanding I turn off the stereo. She's wise to the fact that the next song is Wreck on the Highway and, whether the song cuts out half-way through or not, it's way too close to home for her. All I hear is a good tune but the song takes Leta right back to the night Mike dragged her from the wreck of her own car.

She's in court tomorrow to testify on behalf of her mother who was badly hurt in the crash. Although I knew Mike when the accident happened, we were never close, and rarely in touch, so I hear about it here for the first time, alone and naked with Leta in my attic room. As Leta sketches in the details of the accident, feeling free to talk about it as she never has before, I'm amazed that she's actually here to tell me. The chances were surely higher of them all being killed outright? I try to think back to where I might have been on that night but of course I have no idea. And if Leta had been killed – how could something so huge have happened without my knowing? It's taken a whole year for that night to become a part of my life and there's every possibility I might never have known.

"Guess the name of the policeman," says Leta.

"Which policeman?"

"The policeman at the scene of the accident ... Clint Eastwood. He was so sweet and so kind. He even came to see me in the hospital to make sure I was OK."

Perhaps this is what's bothering me – events like this are more suited to the movies than to real life. The chance that Leta may not have been here to tell me about this accident seems too arbitrary a thing for my life with her to depend upon.

"Clint Eastwood?"

"You don't believe me, do you? Wait and see – he'll be in court tomorrow."

But I don't get to meet Clint Eastwood; I spend most of the next day waiting for Leta in a corridor outside the courtroom. Such is the full and demanding schedule of my life as a writer, I don't mind one bit. The continuing warm weather makes it easy to be doing nothing very much and of course, spending the day in Leta's company – even if I am outside in the corridor of the courthouse, just sat there for over four hours, not even bothering to read, just sat there – means I'm not prey to any insecurities about you know who.

Leta's mother is a beautiful woman but what strikes me most about Maria is the look on her face as she leaves the courtroom. If I catch it right then she thinks it sweet that I should have waited so long for Leta. You know that feeling when you know someone likes you and you like being liked? Well that's Maria for me.

Leta offers to cook me a meal by way of thanks and we buy groceries on the way home from court. As we get back to the house, she asks me a strange question. "You don't fancy my Mum, do you?"

Leta has this way of asking questions that suggests what she really wants, more than anything, is just to make love to you. She wants you to answer the question, sure, and she's interested in what you have to say, but wouldn't it be great to just go upstairs and have sex?

She places the groceries down on the floor and steps across the kitchen to where I'm loading things into the fridge. She puts her arms around me.

"Don't bother putting them away," she says, "I'm about to start cooking."

"Why would I fancy your Mum?" I ask and smile.

"Oh," she says, "all my boyfriends have fancied her at one point or another."

Again, how can I describe the way she talks? Pretending to be hurt? Provocative teasing – you couldn't possibly fancy my Mum more than you do me, could you Gregory?

"Ah, come on," I say. "They were just getting along with her, nothing more than that."

"You don't know because you weren't there."

"You're not telling me that Mike fancied your Mum more than he did you? Or that he was only seeing you so he could get to see your Mum?"

"No, but he fancied her all the same."

"But not to the extent of wanting to do anything about it – "

"I don't know…"

"No way, he was just flirting, being nice."

This is rich: explaining flirting to Leta – she knows no other way to communicate.

"I'm telling you," she says, "he fancied her. He told me."

"Mike told you he fancied your Mum?"

"Yes." Leta smiles.

"And that pissed you off?"

"Yes."

"And what about Sutcliffe?"

"Him too."

I'm tempted to take the opportunity to have a dig at Sutcliffe but I'm big enough to persuade Leta she has them both wrong. She won't have it though and I let it drop. I think it's my general besottedness with all things Leta – as in, I don't fancy *anyone* but Leta – that convinces her I'm not interested in her mother. It's much too nice a day to let such a piece of nonsense bother me. As I write in my diary, Leta and I enjoy a more or less perfect day together. We eat, we share a bath and we go out for the evening.

"Mike wasn't in court," I say later as we get into bed. I'm more than content to talk and fuck all night long. What will I write in my diary tomorrow? 'All I'm interested in is making love and being with Leta.'

"No," says Leta. "Mike sent word to say he had 'pressing business commitments'."

"But you don't think that's the real reason?"

"He's never forgiven me for seeing Sutcliffe when I was supposed to be with him."

"Can you blame him?"

"No," says Leta, "he's right. I wish it hadn't been like that. It was unfair to both of them but particularly hard on Mike."

"Why so for Mike? Why not the same for both?"

"Because Sutcliffe knew the score and besides, we had a different type of relationship; a much more casual arrangement. Mike was still hoping for something more."

"But you weren't?"

"Not with Mike, no."

"And Sutcliffe?"

It's a measure of how good the day is that I have the confidence to ask.

"I didn't have what we have with either Mike or Sutcliffe," she says.

Hearing this and being so close to Leta, I enjoy a rare moment of complete faith and security. But of course she could be lying.

"What about you?" she asks. "Have you ever cheated on anyone?"

"No," I say. I pretend to think about it for a while and then shake my head. "No."

We face each other in the bed and I move my hands along the back of her calves; her body is so perfect.

"Don't," says Leta, "not there."

"What's wrong?"

"Just…something not nice happened when I was younger and that reminds me."

"What?"

"Nothing, forget it."

"No, tell me," I say. This isn't the first time I've noticed something and tonight I feel confident enough to hear anything.

"It's not nice. You won't like me when I tell you."

But it's obvious the whole conversation has been building up to this, perhaps even the whole day. I'm torn between asking and giving her the space to talk.

"My uncle," she says. "When I was fourteen." She speaks so quietly I can barely hear her. "I had to have the baby aborted."

"Which uncle, I mean who…?"

"My Mum's brother."

"And what happened?"

"I told you, we got rid of the baby – do you hate me?"

"No I – why should I hate you? I mean, what happened to your family? How did you all cope?"

"There's only Maria knows about it – oh, and her brother of course. And now you."

"And you never told anyone else?"

"No."

"But what about your uncle? Did you report him to the police?"

"No, we just agreed that he'd never see any of us again."

"And he stuck to that?"

This is so beyond my understanding of how I can conceive of a family to be, that I'm at a loss as to what to say.

In Leta's house you see pictures of the family on the wall, you meet her brothers and sisters and everybody shouts and whistles when Leta asks if you'd like to see her room. In Leta's house, things are so refreshingly normal and happy that you believe in the possibility that one day you will have a family just like this one. And you hope it will be with Leta. But then she tells you this and you know it's going to take a special sort of man for her ever to get over it.

I hope I can be that man but right now I don't know what to make of what she's just told me. I feel protective yes, and can only begin to imagine the pain she's been through, must still be going through. I'm kind of repulsed that someone has done this to Leta – someone I presume she trusted and loved – but if I'm honest then I can see why someone would.

She's crying and I hold her.

"Ssshhh," I say. "Quiet." She's told me now and I realise how important it was she did so. "Let's just sleep for a while," I say.

I feel her wet cheek against my chest. I'm in trouble here; I'm in deep, deeper than I've ever been in my life.

I wonder if she's telling me the truth?

*

If you have a pushbike stolen then you must report it to the police if you hope to claim on the insurance. It's there on the form – 'At which police station did you report your pedal cycle as being stolen?' What the police ask for is the serial number of the bike frame, a number that is barely visible, beneath the crankshaft generally and stamped indelibly into the metal. If you satisfy these two demands then you're likely to receive a payout from the insurance company. When you give the information to the desk clerk at the police station, you both understand that this is as far as it's ever likely to go. If on the outside chance the insurance company do check then it's there in the police files but if you're reporting the bike as stolen in the hope the police are about to go looking for it, then you're likely to be disappointed – no, you will definitely be disappointed.

There's a question on the police form that asks for the colour of the bike and, as you fill in the answer, the desk clerk invariably smiles to himself.

"I don't think it is anymore, somehow, do you?" he'll say and you both have a laugh together because the idea of the police force checking beneath each and every pushbike in Greater Manchester in the hope of seeing your serial number is too ridiculous to contemplate. Not only will your bike not be found; nobody's even going to look for it.

I sold a pushbike in York once because I needed the cash and then a couple of days later I reported it missing in Manchester. I figured they were even less likely to go looking in a different city and so it proved to be; I collected on the insurance. When I visited friends in Oxford, I seriously considered stealing bikes there to sell in Manchester – they seemed to have a more relaxed attitude to security that would make it lucrative and very, very easy. But I held out, I remained strong in my resolve to be a writer.

I think of these things after lunch as I walk into Parrs Wood Police Station to report Caitlin missing. Pushbikes and passports – these are the only reasons I would have willingly entered a police station before now. I don't know if all stations are about the same but any I've seen have that little hatch with a sliding window and a bell on the counter top that you've to ring for attention. I do so and the window opens – both the policeman and myself have to bend down to speak through the gap. You're not talking Fort Apache – The Bronx here, with the desk sergeant high up on his imposing podium; it's more like the off-sales counter down the pub.

"Yes sir, how can I help you?"

"I need to report a missing person," I say.

"Have they been missing long?" he asks,

"Since Monday; about this time on Monday was the last time I saw them – her."

"And what makes you think they – she – may be missing? Is it unusual for this lady to be gone for so long?"

"She didn't come home on Monday night, she didn't go into work yesterday and she didn't come home last night."

"And you're worried?"

"Yes."

"Have you checked with the hospitals?"

"Yes."

"And nothing?"

"No."

"Then really, in my experience you've no need to worry. A lot of people go missing for a day or two and then reappear as though nothing has happened; a little embarrassed maybe, but that's all. I should give it another day or so and I think you'll find she comes home." He's sympathetic but worldly-wise – he's seen to many instances of missing persons that are not really missing, just hiding.

"I'd still like to report her as missing," I say. "Just in case."

"Just in case? In case what? There's not much that can be done at this stage even if she is missing." His initial reassurance, the approach that nearly always works, hasn't allowed him to shut the hatch window and I can see now that he's pissed.

I can't I tell him that the only reason I want to report Caitlin as missing is to feel as though I'm doing something; so that when people ask then I can refer to this and say, see, I reported her as missing? I can go on from here to the school and tell Tomas what I've done and it may reassure him. I won't tell Tomas I have as much hope of the police finding Caitlin as they do a stolen bike but I still know this is the right thing to do.

"Is there anything specific that makes you particularly worried that this lady hasn't come home?" He seems more interested in rubbing his eyes awake with a thumb and forefinger than in hearing the answer to his question.

"I think she was upset," I say.

"But more than that," he replies. "She'd have to be upset to act in any way different to what you'd consider normal. Anything beyond being upset?"

"I don't think she'd ever leave her son," I say.

"You mean, she may have left you but she'd never leave her son?"

"Yes, I guess."

"And you had a row, the last time you saw each other?"

"No, we were getting along fine."

"But you had been fighting at some point recently?"

"We've been having a rough time," I concede, "but nothing to make her up and leave." I don't want to talk about this here with this man. "I think something happened at her workplace on Monday to add to how upset she was and she hasn't been seen since."

"But there you have it," he says. "It can be the smallest of things that set people off and if she was upset then she probably just needs a few days on her own. She knows you're there to look after your son and she's probably hoping you'll understand once she comes home." This is his final shot and he even makes to close the hatch window, smiling his best reassurance as he does so.

"I'm sorry," I say, "but I really do want to report her as missing." He knows I have him because the forty-eight hours have passed but he tries one last shot.

"Have you called all her girlfriends, anyone she may be staying with?"

"I've called anyone I can think of," I say.

"One moment," he says and retreats back into his office, presumably to find a missing persons form. I don't see his face but I see his colleague's. It looks as though they think they have a right one here – this is Gregory out in the world and the world isn't too impressed.

I check my watch and realise that I'm pushing my luck if I want to be in time to pick up Tomas but I know I definitely want to do this. The desk clerk returns with his form.

"What's the name of the person you wish to report as missing?"

I give him Caitlin's full name.

"Could you spell that out for me, please?" And we go through the details of where and when. "And you're married to Mrs. O'Connor?"

"No," I say.

"But you have children together?"

"No, well yes. I mean, she had her son with a different man."

"So what exactly is your relationship to Mrs. O'Connor?"

"I'm her partner," I say.

"Partner – what does that mean? Are you married or not?" he asks.

"No, I said we're not married."

"But you live together?"

"Yes."

"And you look after her son while Mrs. O'Connor's not around? When she goes missing?" At this, he turns fully to his colleague, to make sure his audience is getting all this.

"Look, could you just put my name down as the person reporting her missing? It's the same address as that one there." He does so, still amused. "Is there anything else you need from me?" I ask.

"No sir, I shall process this now." I don't ask what this may mean, practically, in trying to find Caitlin and if anything I'm less optimistic than when I walked in here. "Sir?" he says as I turn to leave.

"Yes?"

"I will process this but you could do yourself a huge favour in the meantime." I wait while he builds himself up for the last word. "If I were you, I would consider the very real possibility that Mrs. O'Connor has dumped you with her son."

"Ms O'Connor," I say. "It's Ms O'Connor."

I run most of the way to school but I'm still late and Tomas is standing by the school doorway with his teacher. I make my apologies but short of giving her the whole story, I'm nothing but a late parent and so beneath her contempt. Tomas is a different matter and I know he must have been going through hell as the playground gradually emptied and I still hadn't arrived. We have tears as soon as we're away from the teacher. I can see that he's really angry at my being so late and I agree; it's unforgivable. Only as I tell him where I've been does he calm down – at the police station reporting his mum missing – as though this is some form of reassurance and consolation. It's all just so crap – I even have to impress on him as I see his hopes rise that little or nothing will come of this, that we're still on our own where his Mum is concerned; we just have to wait and hope she's OK.

As we walk home it occurs to me that Tomas didn't even ask if Caitlin had come home, he just presumed she was still missing.

The burnt-out house is now fully boarded up, as only a council property can be. Our flat looked just the same when Caitlin was first shown where she'd be living; it was impossible to imagine such a place ever being our home. The boards across the windows of the flat, the doors with huge padlocks that were visible from the street and the overgrown grass and weeds in the garden all had the desired effect – this was an undesirable place to be. The message it gave out was that if someone was to take the trouble to break in they'd be bitterly disappointed; this property was not worth even squatting.

The house at number five looks pretty much the same, worse if anything with the blackened walls from the fire. Tomas has stopped mentioning the house as we pass. He probably picked something up from Suzie yesterday that let him know the subject is much too serious to even ask questions or perhaps he's guessed how much I disapprove of Suzie's attitude? We certainly know this house isn't worth squatting in; it's not worth shit now. I wonder if the immediate neighbours were in on the arson? More than likely, I think, when they heard who was moving in next door but never thought the house would go up as it did, underestimated the damage once the fire got out of control. What kind of a people prefer this boarded up waste to a house full of Irish?

As we round the corner Tomas tenses because he sees there's a police car in the street outside our flat. It's not unusual for the street to be visited by the police. It's not even unusual for a police car to be outside our gate, living as we do next door to Suzie who, to be fair, certainly has a bit of previous and, if truth be told, quite a bit of present going on as well. As I have mentioned, Suzie occasionally asks us to mind some of her goods, being, as we are in her eyes, beyond a hint of suspicion from the police. (Not after today though, one visit is all it takes.) When Suzie hands goods over the back fence it's more often than not followed for her by a visit from the law. I don't know how she knows they're about to call but she seems to get it right most of the time. I know it looks odd – why on earth would I get involved in something like this? Especially when I hate the cycle of theft and robbery that plagues the whole estate?

The last time we were broken into then Suzie's son Barry tracked down who had taken the video but was powerless to do anything; it was just some crazy junkie who'd already sold it on for next to nothing. Suzie has little enough time for anyone who robs from their own kind and she regards them as trash. She prefers to aim for a much higher target market but of course, however bad our estate may be, there's always someone worse off than you. So in a way the people that rob off us are just like Suzie, only they don't aim as high. I know I'm in the middle of it – I just don't feel in a position to put a stop to it. So other considerations become more important, like how good Suzie is to us and how essential it is we get along in the neighbourhood. Not much of a justification, I know, but there it is.

Tomas doesn't need to be told the police car is not for Suzie; there's too close a connection to my having reported his Mum missing and too much on his mind for it to mean anything else. His grip tightens in my hand and as we walk he moves his body in closer to my own. I'm not prepared here – I forgot to imagine the worst as we came round the corner, distracted by the house fire – and maybe now the worst has arrived.

A policeman gets out the driver's side of the car, a policewoman out the passenger side. They've been waiting.

"Mr O'Connor?" the policeman asks.

"No, I – is it about Caitlin?"

"Do you mind if we have a few words – inside?"

Suzie calls from her doorway.

"Do you want me to take Tomas, Gregory?"

Tomas is practically attached to my side at this stage and I ignore them all as I kneel down to speak to him. I do however catch a smirk from the policeman, aimed at Suzie and the very idea of someone giving their kids for her to mind – I don't catch Suzie's reaction. Tomas' face is a deep red and he looks set to burst into tears again. I put my hands firmly on his shoulders.

"I don't know what these police are going to say, Tomas. It's obviously something about your Mum and I can't imagine it's very good."

"Do you think she –?"

"I really don't know but let's face it, only when we see your Mum at home again will everything be OK. Now I said we were in this together, so I'm going to give you the choice – do you want to come with me and speak to them or do you want to go to Suzie's house?"

"Stay with you." No contest.

"OK," I say, "but remember, anything we have to face then we face together." Tomas nods in agreement and I stand up. "Thanks Suzie," I call over, "he's fine."

We walk through the gate to the flat. There are so many things going through my head it's impossible to think clearly but I do pick up a sense that the policeman's attitude is not of someone come to deliver bad news. The presence of a policewoman however is worrying; I don't know why she would be here if not to soften the blow. As ever, there's also my own nervousness in the company of the law, enough for me to have difficulty with the key in the lock. I know they're watching me struggle and it makes me fumble more. Once inside we all four stand in the living room until I suggest they should sit. I don't like the police, I don't want them in my home and I don't want this to be happening. Tomas stands by my side as I sit on the edge of the seat of the armchair. The other two are similarly perched on the sofa. The policeman turns off his radio and the policewoman takes out a notepad. They begin.

"Do you know of a Caitlin O'Connor, sir?" It's him that asks the question; naturally he pronounces the name wrong but now is not the time.

"Yes," I say, "she lives here."

"Do you have any idea of her whereabouts?" he asks.

"What – I mean, pardon?" I say.

"Do you know where she might be?"

"No, of course not. I've just come from the police station. I reported her missing about an hour ago." They look at each other.

"Which station was this?" he asks.

"Parrs Wood, about an hour ago. You mean you didn't know? Have you found her?"

He looks to the policewoman and nods. She stands up and leaves the room to talk into her radio. It doesn't take a genius to guess where she's calling. "You're checking?"

"It will only take a moment to verify, sir."

"But why would you want to check to see if I've reported her missing? Do you know where she is?" I see the look on his face, supposedly non-committal but actually quite stupid. "You don't know, do you?" Tomas moves his body slightly away to look at me, to see what this means. Is this good news or bad? "If you don't know where she is," I ask the copper, "then why are you here?"

"It will only take a moment, sir," he repeats and sure enough in comes the policewoman. Now it's she that nods to him, this time to confirm my story.

"Why would you report Mrs. O'Connor missing?"

"Miss," I say wearily. "Ms, actually."

"Pardon, sir?"

"Ms O'Connor; we're not married."

"But you're Mr O'Connor, no?"

"No, I just couldn't be bothered correcting you out at the car," I say. "What are you doing here if you don't know where she is?"

"If you don't mind, sir." At least he stops short of saying he'll ask the questions. "Why did you report Miss O'Connor as missing this afternoon?"

"Because she is and we're worried. We thought the police might be able to help."

"No, why this afternoon? Why not earlier?"

"Because it's just forty-eight hours since I last saw her and you, as in the police, don't acknowledge anyone as missing until that time has passed; surely you know that?"

"But is it normal that you wouldn't see Miss O'Connor for such a long period? Weren't you worried earlier?"

"Yes, I've been worried since Monday evening but what could I do?"

"And she gave you no indication that she would be away from home for such a length of time?"

"No, if she had then I wouldn't be worried and I wouldn't have reported her missing. Look, why are you here exactly?" The policewoman checks her colleague with her hand.

"Perhaps we should start from the beginning," she says.

"What's happening?" asks Tomas. "Do they know where my Mum is?"

"No, son, they don't know. I think they've come about something else. Do you want to stay here while I see what they want?" Again, he answers by pushing his head in close against my upper arm.

"Your name, sir?" She's taken over the questions – fact gathering.

"Gregory, Gregory Isaacs."

"Like the singer?"

"Yes, like the singer," I agree.

"And you're not married to Miss, sorry, Ms O'Connor?"

"No."

"But you do live here?"

"Yes."

"And this is your son?"

"Yes, no – I'm his Dad, not his natural father."

"What does that mean?" asks the policeman and I look at him.

"I'm his Dad, not his natural father."

"OK," interjects the policewoman, "and the boy's – Tomas's, right? – Tomas's natural father – "

"Hasn't had any contact with him since he was born," I say. None of this is news to Tomas but it's still not good to be quizzed on it in front of him. I look to the policewoman and I try to get this across. It's too late to decide now that Tomas is better off next door with Suzie. Thankfully, the policewoman changes tack.

"You say there's no reason that you know of that Ms O'Connor would have gone missing?"

"I haven't seen her since Monday lunchtime when she said she'd be straight home after work."

"But she never came home?"

"No."

"And no arguments, no falling-out that would give her reason to stay away?"

"No, we were getting on fine."

"Then why do you think –?"

"I don't know. She's been upset ..." I begin.

"Why upset?" she asks.

"Nothing, personal stuff. We've had some bad news recently and she's been upset over that."

"What news?" It's him again and there comes to be a point

where your deference to the police has a limit.

"None of your business," I say.

Once again she steps in.

"What do you do, Mr Isaacs?"

"Do? You mean work?"

"Yes."

"I – I'm a writer."

"A writer?"

"What do you write?" he asks.

"Stories," I say.

"And does that pay?" he asks. I ignore him.

"Mr Isaacs," says the policewoman. "You write for a living? How do you make your money – do you sell your stories?"

"I operate as a self-employed business. I have a weekly grant from the government and I also supplement that by taking in typing work."

"He's on the dole," says the policeman. "I knew it, they're all the same." He starts looking around the room, checking out the stereo, telly, video, the sofa he's sat upon.

"You take in work from students, is it?" she asks.

"Mainly," I say, "typing up their theses and essays."

"And that's allowed by the scheme you're on?"

Where the fuck are they going with all this? We're a long way from finding Caitlin, that's for sure but I know enough to know I can't win here so I answer the questions.

"I'm given a weekly grant," I repeat. "I have to declare that as income in my accounts for the taxman at the end of the financial year."

"But it's fair to say that Ms O'Connor is the main earner in the household?"

"Yes, she earns more money than I do."

"But you have responsibility for Tomas here while Ms O'Connor is at work?"

"Or missing?" he adds.

"Yes, I'm responsible for looking after Tomas, picking him up from school, things like that."

"Like a 'house husband'?" It's a new phrase and he injects

it with as much ridicule as possible.

"Yes, like a house husband," I say.

"So she goes off for a few days, safe in the knowledge that her kid is being looked after by you? Nice arrangement."

"Yes," I say again, "she can go off for as long as she likes, safe in the knowledge that Tomas is being looked after by me. It's called a partnership."

"Yeah, right! Wise up chump!"

"Mr Isaacs." It's her again. "Is Ms O'Connor Irish?"

As she asks the question, I immediately make the connection. Caitlin sees the Irish family on Monday, they wreck the place on Tuesday and Caitlin's still missing by Wednesday. They're here for the low-down on Caitlin. Ann was right about their line of reasoning and at least I know now why they're here.

"Irish?" I say.

"Yes, Irish," the policewoman repeats.

"She was born in Manchester," I say.

"But she would be from an Irish family, with a name like O'Connor?"

"Who isn't from an Irish family around here?"

"I'm not," says the policeman.

"No," I say. "I guess not. Caitlin's English."

"Then why do you pronounce her name like that – like Cat instead of Kate?"

"Because that's her name."

"Strange spelling."

"That's because it's an Irish name – excellent detective work. She was born in Manchester, in St. Mary's, the same place as Tomas."

I immediately regret mentioning Tomas as the filth turns his attention to where Tomas is stood by my side. He is the filth; it may be just a name but he is the filth. This is why I didn't want them in my home; they think that everybody they come across is scum. This is what everybody learns – that at any given moment the police can fuck you over and that they're more than likely to the first chance they get.

"But it would be fair to say," interrupts the policewoman, "that she would have sympathies with the Irish?"

"It depends on her options," I say looking at the filth.

"Mr Isaacs, there was a very serious incident at your partner's workplace yesterday and we believe that Ms O'Connor was in some way involved."

"You mean somebody trashed the place when they realised they wouldn't be given a new house?" I say.

"What do you know of it?" she asks.

"Oh for Christ's sake," I say, "just what everybody around here knows – they were burnt out on Sunday night before they'd even moved in and went back to the Social on Monday. When they were given nothing they went back in force on Tuesday to trash the place. What else is there to know?"

A clearer picture is starting to form in my head – that of Caitlin dealing with this case on her first day back at work. I can't imagine much sympathy being shown to this family by the Department and Caitlin was probably alone in at least trying to help them.

"Well," says the policewoman, "we know the Burke family won't be troubling us again, not for a while at least. What we'd like to know is Ms O'Connor's part in all this and it's a little difficult, given that she's gone missing on us all."

"I'd say she was given the job of telling them they were fucked – "

"Mr Isaacs – "

"I'd say she was given the job of informing them that despite the fact their house was burnt to the ground then the Department could do no more to help them at this stage."

"You were recorded on videotape as being at the back entrance of the building yesterday morning. What were you doing there?"

"Checking to see if Caitlin had arrived at work – Jesus!" I had no idea that back entrance was on camera. It's amazing how the simplest of actions can be made to look suspicious.

"You don't think Caitlin may have disappeared for her own personal reasons?" I ask. "It has to be suspicious that she's gone missing?"

"Well," says the policewoman, "you're not being too

forthcoming on any other reasons…"

"She's been upset, I told you. I guess things got to be too much for her. If I told you her father had died, would that help you at all?"

"Has he?"

"No."

"Then why would you say such a thing?"

"Because it could be as simple an explanation as that. Instead you call here checking to see if I'm claiming dole while Caitlin's working at the Social; to see if there's any dirt on Caitlin. Let me guess, someone made a bad decision and they're pointing the finger at her?"

"Then why not just give us a full explanation for her disappearance?" she asks.

"Because I don't know for one and even if I did, I'm not sure I would with him here." I look over at the filth sat on my sofa; I really resent him being in my home. "Do us all a favour," I say, "and just find her. Then you have your explanation"

"I'll give you an explanation," says the filth standing. "She's dumped you with her kid here and probably fucked off back to Ireland where she belongs. Along with that scum of a family, is my bet. Come on," he says to his colleague, "we'll get nothing from this sap. Let's leave him to his house-husbanding." The policewoman folds up her notebook, stands and mumbles her thanks and then they're gone.

I'm left sitting in the living room, with Tomas by my side.

"Well," I say, "that went well, don't you think?" But flippancy is wrong for Tomas – all he sees is his Dad arguing with the police and even less chance of his Mum ever coming home.

"What happened?" he asks. "Will they find my Mum?"

"I think they know less than we do, son. We're back to where we started – we have to believe your Mum knows what she's doing."

At this Tomas cries – deep sobs from inside his little body – and I let him. Enough with being strong, I think, just let out as much as you can. But he stops as quickly as he starts, as though he realises even this will do him no good.

"Come on champ," I say, "let's get you something to eat. Here, wipe your eyes." I pass him a tissue.

"OK chump," he says with a brave smile.

"You heard that, did you? He wasn't too nice, was he?"

"No," Tomas agrees and we go through to the kitchen together. My hands are shaking as I prepare some food for Tomas and make a cup of tea for myself. It's always like this after coming into contact with the filth. I sit down with Tomas but I'm unable to drink the tea for the tremor in my hands. I don't want to make it so obvious to Tomas so I put the cup down while I try to calm my breathing. I think I may be sick but when I go through to the bathroom it's just a trembling in my belly and no serious retching; I go back to Tomas in the kitchen. I see Suzie over the fence out the back, trying to catch my attention. When I open the back door she asks in a hushed voice,

"Have they gone?"

"Yes, they're gone," I say.

"What did they want?" she asks in a more normal tone. "Was it about Caitlin?" Hushed again as she looks through to see that Tomas is listening.

"Yes," I say, "but they don't know where she might be. It was more to do with what happened at the Social yesterday, like Caitlin had something to do with it."

"Stupid bastards," she says. I expect to get another stream of shit about Irish knackers but Suzie must have picked something up from me yesterday and lets it pass – it's not the same without a sympathetic audience.

"Still no sign of her then?" she asks.

"No," I reply. I look at the pushbike in Suzie's back yard. I've been intending to ask her son Barry about it for a while now. I know it's a good bike and he doesn't seem to be doing much with it – I'm sure he'd give it to me at a low price if I asked.

"She'll be back, Gregory, don't you worry. We all go off the rails at one time or another." She indicates by nodding her head to the side that she wants to speak to me away from Tomas' hearing. I can't shut the door on him but I do walk a little way down the garden. "I can't have them coming around here, Gregory," says Suzie.

"Sorry?"

"I can't have them calling without warning." I realise she's talking about the police and when I look at her face I can see she's in deadly earnest.

"I don't think they'll call again," I say feebly. How the fuck do I know what the filth are going to do?

"Well, I'm just saying. I've enough trouble with them as it is, especially that cunt that was here today, if you'll pardon my language only that's what he is." She nods her head to confirm it. I've been warned.

We receive only the one phone call throughout the evening and it's from my friend Roger. The house is so quiet with just the two of us that I allow Tomas more than his usual hour of TV. Not only is Caitlin not here, but also it's also obvious to Tomas that no one is about to phone. I guess all Caitlin's friends presume that if she was home then she'd be on to them to put their minds at rest ('Silly Gregory, I told him I was going away for a few days.') and they'll just get me if they ring. I don't get on with them well enough for them to want to speak to me, especially about something as awkward as this. Still, you'd think someone would call, if only to ask? Not that I'm complaining – if Ann was representative last night of how supportive Caitlin's friends can be then I'm OK without that kind of help. And the famous Rosie and Bill – does their concern not extend as far as a phone call? Or are they also presuming that Caitlin will call to let them know she's safe? Where does that leave their opinion of me? Perhaps she's called them and told them where she is but they've agreed not to say?

Tomas looks up from the TV when the phone rings but looks back to the screen when he realises who's on the line.

"Gregory, it's Roger – any news?"

"No, nothing," I say. "Well, not unless you call a visit from the police to be news." I explain what happened and what I believe the police were thinking but how they're so far wide of the mark where Caitlin's concerned.

"What, that Caitlin told them to go back in on Tuesday morning and wreck the place?" asks Roger.

"Exactly," I say, "and then goes missing because she knows she's in trouble – completely off the wall."

"But whatever happened," continues Roger, "on Monday, I mean, whatever happened is probably what has tipped Caitlin – ". He stops before saying 'over the edge'.

I agree; I think that what happened to that family was too much for Caitlin to handle.

"But it still doesn't tell us where she might be," I say.

"No," agrees Roger. "Look, the reason I'm calling, apart from, you know, to see if there's any news, is to say that Mary checked with the hospitals again today and there was nothing." He's quiet for a moment, as though deciding whether to continue and then he does so. "And Mary said, before she went to work and I think I agree with her, that if Caitlin isn't with any of her friends and if she hasn't called by tonight, then you've got to start thinking the worst."

"It doesn't seem to make much difference what I think," I say.

"You know what I mean."

"Yes, I do and I appreciate you saying it but really, I've reported it to the police – I don't know what else there is to do but wait."

"Mary says, and again I agree with her, that Caitlin took the news from the hospital harder than you think."

I don't know how much harder she could have taken it.

"Gregory, are you there?"

"Yes."

"We think you've got to accept the possibility that she may have done something to herself. Damaged herself in some way," he adds.

"But they'd still have to find her body," I say and wince as I realise what I've just said. I look across at Tomas and hope he's as engrossed in the TV as he appears to be.

"Yes," he agrees, "sooner or later. You can't think where she might go?"

"No."

"Her parents?"

"No, there's just no way – besides, short of looking up all the O'Connor's in the phone book, I wouldn't know where to start."

"It may come to that," says Roger.

"I don't think so," I say. "I really don't."

"Call me if you need anything."

"I will. And Roger," I add, "I appreciate you calling."

"No worries – take care."

There's little else to do but to get Tomas ready and into bed. As he's sleeping with me again tonight, it's not long before I join him. What else are we to do? Even this, it seems, can become a routine.

The attic room is hot, too hot in summer and almost unbearable today because I have a fever that's out of control. I've been sick for the previous two nights and the heat of the day won't allow me to recover. I'm in a twilight world of credible nightmares; long, tedious and boring scenarios that my mind goes over and over before I realise I'm dreaming and the wave of nausea returns. It's so fucking lonely – Roger and Mary are away on holiday and I haven't seen or spoken to anyone since the cramps first took hold of my stomach – not unless you count Leta's voice on her answer machine. I know it's just a question of time, that the fever will pass, but every minute takes an eternity and so I try not to check my watch but when I do I see that nothing has changed.

Then I hear the key in the door downstairs and I thank God because I know straight away it can only be Leta. I ignore the question of why she took so long to arrive, I'm just so grateful now she's here.

"I heard there's a patient by the name of Gregory," she says laughing as she puts her head around the door. It's a Gregory

Isaacs song that's been playing all summer.

"My Night Nurse," I say with a weak smile.

"Jesus, Gregory, get some air in here, can't you?" She looks at the wide-open window and runs back downstairs to create a draught by opening the other windows below. I immediately feel the benefit of a slight breeze. As Leta returns to the attic room, I'm conscious of how I must appear; such a contrast to her vitality, her summer clothes and sunglasses pushed back in her hair.

"You've got to get out of here," she says and immediately she regrets it – memories of Sutcliffe and TB and missed birthdays. "I mean, you go and get a wash and I'll change your sheets." I get up out the bed, happy for Leta to take charge but my legs feel weak and I hate to look like this while she's here. "And here," she says, "take off that night shirt and find something clean to wear." I slowly make my way to the bathroom, already feeling as though the fever may be beaten by these few simple measures. But as I return to my room I have to fall immediately onto the bed so I don't pass out and I know I'm not through this yet.

"There's fresh water here," says Leta, "and fruit and biscuits for when you're ready to eat. I'll call you in a couple of days."

"Are you leaving?" I ask. I know I'm not much of an attraction here but I can't believe this.

"I've friends downstairs in the car. I insisted we came over when I picked up your call but they're waiting on me now."

"Friends?"

"Yes Gregory, friends. Don't do this – "

"When did you pick up the message – just now?" But she's ahead of me.

"I've been staying at home for a few days. I went back to the flat to pick up some things after lunch and there you were, crying out for help. Crying out for your Night Nurse." She picks up my hand. "And here I am – but I must run; there's not much more I can do here now anyway." A squeeze of my hand and she's gone.

If I'm honest then this is the moment I know for certain.

I know she's been staying at Sutcliffe's; he's waiting for Leta in the car downstairs. Despite myself I stand on the bed to look out my attic window but the angle of the roof obscures the view of the road. The Mad Detective – I've read about him in books and I've seen him in my friends; now I have become him and he'll never let me be.

I know it's over with Leta but of course I don't want to believe it and if I can just get well then, maybe I'm wrong and everything will be OK? So I lie back in my clean sheets.

Over the coming months the evidence, as they say, is compelling, and I know that whatever Leta was looking for, she couldn't find in me.

Of course, it drags on; there are many scenes still to come. While we're away on holiday, Leta leaves the hotel to call home rather than call from our room. We both know why and though he's like a physical presence with us throughout the holiday, neither of us mention Sutcliffe's name. Only when we get home, when it's so bleedingly obvious that Sutcliffe is back in her life – as in, his clothes are in her room when I call – do I finally admit what I'd refused to believe.

And then I think – if she was lying about that then when did she tell me the truth? Clint Eastwood? Look at the diary entry and note the day – April 1st – April Fools' Day. Leta's mother smiled at me that day as she left the courtroom and it made me feel good, but what did she really see? Was I a sap even then? I have it written down in my diary but was that really such a perfect day after all? Was it really as I remember it, or even as I thought it to be at the time? Were Leta and I really that close, were we really in love or was I already being used? April Fool – who knows?

So when Leta writes a letter after several months to tell me her body 'feels wretched and ugly' without me, then I keep that letter to remind me of how I feel. I still have the letter but it's the time I spend alone in my sickbed that I hold on to. I tell myself that I'll never go back to those days of deceit, of not knowing the truth from the lies and of feeling so completely alone. So when Leta and I meet for one last time, after she writes and I don't reply to her letter, when she calls to my attic room to see me and we make love – and I remember even now how it feels to be coming inside her, as though my whole being is pouring into this one woman – even this one last time we both know I can never go back.

Six

I can't say whether it's for my sake or for Tomas's but we stay at home on Thursday morning. It's not tiredness – we've both slept well the past two nights, each finding some comfort in the other sleeping in the same bed – though we do take our time to get up once the decision is made. I don't know, the thought of repeating yesterday – the sense of uselessness, going through the motions, doing only what I feel obliged to do but knowing it will have absolutely no effect, being late for picking up Tomas at school – I don't want to go through all that again. Perhaps I'm using Tomas but he agrees so readily to staying at home there has to be some good in this? It's unthinkable to Tomas that his mother won't come home eventually so naturally he wants to be here when she does. My initial intention of carrying on as normal has worn thin after only a couple of days; for all the difference it has on whether Caitlin comes home, it really doesn't matter what I do.

"I'll call the school at nine," I say and we snuggle down together beneath the bedclothes. It's warm in here and we giggle together at the sheer luxury of this compared to the cold walk to school. I know it's the right decision when I see Tomas' reaction. It's not as though he dislikes school – in fact the opposite is true – but surely these are exceptional circumstances? And doing something for ourselves, not just what the world would expect us to do – it makes us feel good.

Tomas is eating his cereal in the living room, in front of the telly. He never does this on a school day, only occasionally at the weekend while Caitlin and I spend time together in bed. So it's a treat, a concession, a nod to what he must be going through. I've gone back to bed. I love my time with Tomas but I need time on my own to think clearly, to try to figure out what I should do next. Even if no startling revelations occur to me, which they don't, just the time spent alone helps to calm me down. There's no explanation here that I can see and, as Roger had said last night, I have to start thinking the unthinkable. And he's right; Caitlin's more likely to have done something to herself rather than to have had something done to her.

There's a knock at the door. Tomas is all for answering it immediately in his pyjamas but I stop him while I quickly get dressed. It's more than likely Suzie or, knowing my luck, Olivia, calling when Tomas would normally be in school. Tomas stands beside me as I open the door but it's no one I know.

"Mr Isaacs?" It's a middle-aged woman, smartly dressed, and she checks some notes on her file as she asks me my name. I'm reminded of Caitlin's nun, the one I dodged at the door and eventually had to allow through; maybe she's come back in plain clothes to fool some more money out of us? Whoever, it's just some official calling to our door and I tell Tomas to go back inside before he catches cold.

"Mr Isaacs?" she asks again, this time looking up and directly at me. I'm reluctant to reply because I'm not officially resident here – as in, who official would know that I live here?

"Yes," I confirm after a second or two.

"I'm from the Social Services." She holds up her I.D. "I've come to talk to you about Tomas O'Connor."

This is the moment, like with the nun, that she expects to be asked to come in or allowed through.

"I think you'd better call back," I say. "Tomas's mother isn't here. It would be her you'd need to talk to."

"Oh no," she says, " I know Ms O'Connor's not here; that's why I need to talk to you."

Her tone is light and breezy, with no awareness of the effect her words might be having.

"How do you know that Ms O'Connor's not here?" I ask.

"But she's not, is she?" she counters as though this plain matter of fact is so obvious she can't understand why we're discussing it. "I just need to ask you a few questions about Tomas."

"OK," I nod and this really pisses her off.

"Mr Isaacs, our primary concern here is the welfare of – "

"You mean you want to come inside?" I ask.

"Yes," she says. "If you don't mind."

I open the door fully and she walks through to the living room.

"Sit down," I say and offer her coffee. "Tomas, I'm sorry but the telly has to go off while I talk to this lady – "

"Marsha," she smiles. "Tomas, isn't it?"

I leave them be while I make some coffee in the kitchen. I'm not stupid – I know I have to be seen to cooperate as much as possible with this woman, whatever the reason for her calling. I know that without Caitlin here I have to be careful and I take time making the coffee so I can compose myself. But this still doesn't prepare me for the crassness of what she's about to say.

"Mr Isaacs," she says after I bring through the coffee, "we have to discuss who will be responsible for Tomas in the continued absence of Ms O'Connor."

"Sorry, one second," I say. "Tomas, could you go through to get dressed?" He looks at me reluctantly but I insist. "And washed," I add as he leaves the room. I realise I'm not washed yet; I reach over to the desk for my glasses so that at the very least I can see this woman, this Marsha.

"Sorry." She smiles apologetically as though this is something she comes across every day. "This can't be easy for you?"

"Isn't it a little early to be reckoning on Caitlin not coming back?" I ask. What is she doing here? Is this visit a direct result of my reporting Caitlin missing yesterday? Have I invited this extra piece of shit into my life or was it the filth calling yesterday and then tipping off the Social Services?

"I think we have to be ready for whatever may happen," she says. "I know it's difficult but you must think of Tomas." Christ, it's like being back at the hospital – any minute now she's going to ask me how I feel about things.

"I do think of Tomas," I say. "I am thinking of Tomas and I don't think you being here – suggesting that his mother might never come home – I can't see how that could be doing him any good. Why are you here, anyway?" I ask. "I mean, why now?"

"Well, as I – "

"No," I say, "I mean, if Tomas's welfare is uppermost in your mind then what good did you think it would do to come here?"

"Well, I…I didn't expect Tomas to be here, to tell you the truth. By rights he should be at school."

"I kept him off school today," I say. It's really hard not to react. Everything about this woman is alien to me – her accent, her make-up, her rings and jewellery, her shoes, her briefcase. What does she know of me and my world? Where was she when Caitlin and Tomas really needed her, or at least one of her colleagues? Caitlin once described to me her sense of aloneness after Tomas was first born, her desolation and her feelings of uselessness. She told me there was more than one occasion when she had to leave Tomas crying alone in the sheltered accommodation while she walked the streets for fear of doing him harm out of frustration. That was when she needed help, not here and now. I think this is the first ever visit from Social Services since Tomas was born.

"If Ms O'Connor remains missing, then custody of Tomas would pass to ourselves." There's no stopping her. "I'm right in thinking that you're not married?"

"No, we're not married."

"Then it would be up to the Department to decide what is in Tomas's best interests."

"But he lives he with me," I say. "Surely that's the best thing for Tomas, to continue with what he knows?"

"We would take that into consideration, naturally, but there are other matters to consider."

"Such as?"

"Well, there would be his natural father for a start – "

"You're kidding," I say.

"No," she says looking up from her notes. "We would have to consider all possibilities."

"But surely you know there's a whole history there?" I can't say too much because I know Tomas is listening but it's inconceivable they would consider Imran as a suitable guardian for Tomas.

"We would have to take into account the rights of everybody concerned," she says. "To be quite honest with you Mr Isaacs, Tomas's father would have a far greater legal claim than yourself."

What are we talking about here? Let's call it as it is: what's going to happen to Tomas if Caitlin never comes back, if Caitlin is dead?

"You can't be serious," I say. "I mean, not about me but about him. There's a barring order on him to keep away from Tomas and Caitlin."

"From Ms O'Connor only, I think you'll find," she says. "We would have to think long and hard about this case. There's also the fact that it's Tomas's mother who's missing here. It's not healthy for a child to be without at least some form of female care."

"But it would be OK for him to be without his dad?" I ask.

"And while–" she continues, as if I had not spoken, "and while it's obvious that you care and look after Tomas, we would take a dim view of him, for example, not attending school."

I don't believe this.

"We shall contact Tomas's father if Ms O'Connor remains listed as missing."

"But she's only been gone a couple of days," I say.

"And hopefully she'll turn up and everything will be as before. We shall be keeping in close contact with the police who I believe are looking for Ms O'Connor?"

"Yes."

"And in the meantime if you could try to ensure that Tomas is well cared for and keeps to his daily routine as much as possible."

"You mean, make sure he goes to school every day?"

"Well that, and…"

"And what?"

"Be conscious of his welfare, who takes care of him when he's not with you, things like that."

"Don't leave him with neighbours?"

"Only if you think those neighbours are suitable," she says, leaving me in no doubt where she stands on that one. "Now." She puts her file in her briefcase and stands up. "I only say these things for – "

"For Tomas's welfare, I know."

"No, I was going to say for your own sake. It's in your best interests should we ever come to the point where we have to decide what will happen to Tomas."

And she's gone. I guess I'm taking Tomas to school after all.

Dropping Tomas at school part way through the day reminds me of that first week when I waited inside the corridor to collect him. It's like we enter a closed world, recognisable and acceptable to Tomas but strange and excluding to me. As it's almost midday, I'm tempted to wait for the lunch-break and let Tomas mingle in unnoticed amongst his friends in the playground but I know that wouldn't be right. As we enter the school, Tomas is all for running straight down to his classroom but again I know I have to inform someone of his arrival and I don't wish to do this in front of the whole class.

"Where's the office?" I ask Tomas but already our being there has caught the head teacher's attention. Her door opens and she removes her reading glasses as she walks towards us. I start to explain why Tomas is only now arriving at school.

"That's quite alright," she says, coldly I feel. "I was told Tomas was on his way."

"Told?"

"Tomas, you can go on down to your classroom now."

He walks off but I call him back to kiss him goodbye.

"See you at home time," I say and hug him. He does a tiny little wave as he disappears into his class. The head and myself are left alone in the corridor.

"Mr O'Connor," she says, "you do realise it's an offence

not to bring your child to school."

"Yes, I – "

"Without good reason, of course."

"I thought I had good reason," I say.

"And what was that?" she asks.

What do I say? That his mother's gone missing? It sounds as though Social Services have already been in touch with the school. I think that whatever I say isn't going to be good enough for this woman and I'm not in a position to argue, not without alienating her towards Tomas. I shake my head.

"I would say that as his parent then it's up to me to decide whether Tomas is fit to come to school," I say. "It's up to me to decide if for one day he's better off at home."

"But you're not, are you?"

"Not what?"

"Not Tomas's parent, so in this case it's not up to you to decide."

"No, I'm not his natural father," I say, "is that what you mean?" I take a step towards her and she steps back. "But I am his parent, I'm more than just *loco parentis*, and whether I am or not is not for you to decide but for Tomas's mother, only we can't ask her because no one's got the first fucking idea where she is right now."

"Mr O'Connor, you can't use language like that to me. Now please leave."

Every time. They fall back on the language thing every time. The language and not the argument becomes the issue and of course, I never learn.

"You don't even know my fucking name but you think you have the right to tell me how to look after my son," is what I want to say.

"My name's not O'Connor," is what I do say. I walk away down the corridor and out the school.

The police are no longer outside Caitlin's workplace so I ring the bell by the staff entrance. I'd try to figure out where the cameras are hidden but I realise this would seem suspicious.

Frank takes his time to answer but thankfully recognises me when he sees me through the glass mesh door. Instead of going to open the door as he has on the countless other occasions I've been wanting to let Caitlin know I've arrived, he moves to the side to press a new intercom button. He looks his age as he scrutinises how to work the new system. His voice comes through shaky and unsure.

"Yes?" And then louder, "Yes?"

"Frank, it's Gregory – Caitlin's partner?"

"Yes?" He looks at the intercom rather than through the door to me.

"I just wanted to check," I say, "if you've heard anything from her? If she's called in to work at all?" Talk about clutching at straws.

"No, I…no," he says.

"Is it possible to have a word with Ann? Maybe she would know something?" I'm bawling this through the door. I haven't a clue if he can hear me clearly or not.

"Can't do that," he says. "You'll have to call around to the front desk. 'This door not to be opened to any member of the public.'" He points to a sign by the intercom.

"OK, thanks," I say. Frank shuffles off. I'm not sure there's any use in calling to the front desk. I could always wait here for the staff to emerge for their lunch breaks, whether it's Ann or anyone else I recognise, but there's something so pathetically desperate about it I decide against this idea. Similarly, trying to come across Caitlin's workmates by chance while they're out at lunch – what am I thinking of?

I walk through the alleyway to the public entrance; they have an initial reception desk that fields callers and directs them to the correct queue. I ask to speak to Ann – perhaps she's calmed down a little after the other day?

"What's it about?" asks the receptionist.

"It's just a personal call," I say. "If you could just call up to her to say that Gregory's here."

"I can't do that," she says. "If it's a personal call then you'll have to dial through on her direct line. If not then you'll have to wait in line to be seen."

"I was just passing," I say. "Could you not just call up to her and tell her I'm here?"

"Sorry," she says, "new guidelines."

I look at the waiting area – it's like a fucking zoo as usual, probably worse for being closed the other day. There's no way I'm going in there, only to be told they've heard nothing, or heard nothing they're prepared to tell me. I vaguely wander outside, unsure now what to do – it's hardly worth my while walking home only to double back for the end of the school day. I'm hungry but not sure of where or what to eat. I decide to go along to Safeway, get some food in for this evening, and then wait around for Tomas.

I pick up a basket and I've walked the length of the first aisle before seriously considering what I should buy. So far this week, Tomas and I have made do with whatever was in the house, other things being on our minds and all. I try to think what I need and continue to walk down the aisles. I have no idea what I should cook for us this evening. It seems so pointless. I pick something from the shelf in front of me – a tin of tuna – and put it in my basket. I could cook some pasta and use the tuna in a sauce. Should I buy a sauce or make one myself? I can't remember if we have enough spaghetti but it's not expensive and we'll get to use it eventually. We've got onions, though I know Tomas hates onions, but I'm not going to cook a sauce without using onions but then I need to buy some tinned tomatoes and he hates them too so fuck that, I'll just buy a ready-made sauce but they're a fucking rip-off and what would go with tuna anyway? So I dump the tuna on a different shelf because, come to think of it, I don't think he likes that either. A blindness comes over me; I can see but I can't make out what's on the shelf in front of me. I wheel around, still with an empty basket and lean on a freezer cabinet. Frozen fish, in breadcrumbs – we both like that. If I get some spuds, yes, that's easier and some baked beans and I know he hasn't had any green veg for days but if I buy some apples then that would do it. I realise I'm crying and even though I know

I've become a crazy, I don't care because I'm giving in, OK you cunts you've won. I'm just another crazy in Safeway's, nothing new there. I make my way to the check-out and try to find an empty one to go through but they've all got chains across so I walk along to the end where I can get out anyway, walk all the way back to the exit, dropping my basket in a pile by the door.

Outside, there are seats along the wall and although it's cold, it's undercover and dry, out the wind and a place to be without having to make any decisions. I really don't want to walk home just to have to walk back again so I stay here for a while, for quite a while actually, and think of nothing. I close my eyes and feel weary enough to sleep; maybe I do sleep. If anyone sees me they can think what they will, it's the least of my problems I like hearing the noise of people go by that I have no connection to or responsibility for. I check my watch and am surprised by how quickly the time has passed and I decide not to sink back into the sleepiness for fear of being late for Tomas. I don't feel quite so desperate – Tomas saves me once again, at least somebody needs me – but I don't go back into Safeway's, just in case.

I'm early when I arrive back at the school and I wait for a few other parents to gather by the doorway before walking across the playground. I'm not interested in continuing my conversation with the head teacher should she be around. Once the kids start to emerge though, it's just like any other school day. Tomas quickly checks I'm there and then struggles to put on his coat while still holding his bag.

"Here," I say and reach out for his bag. While I wait for him to button up I notice three men walk across to a group of parents and ask for directions. The parents point our way and I look behind me to see what it is they're talking about but it's obviously us. The parents turn away as they see me notice but continue to talk to the three men. As we leave the playground, I'm conscious of being watched and talked about.

The filth are there at our gate again as we arrive home from school. It's turning into something of a daily occurrence for the locals who are out in force now to witness events at first hand. Even Harry the Horse – so called, I don't know why – is up and out his bed by four in the afternoon, an event in itself. Harry is famous locally, not only for his laziness and sleeping habits, but for applying to manage Queen of the South soccer team when they recently advertised in the Manchester Evening News. I didn't see who eventually got the job but I wasn't surprised when Harry wasn't invited to an interview; let's just say his skills on the soccer pitch are somewhat less than silky. It's an honour that his wife should consider it worth her while to disturb Harry from his late afternoon nap.

Unlike yesterday, Tomas is not fooled into thinking the presence of the police might mean some progress in finding his Mum – how our little impressions are formed – and is more immediately concerned with my reaction.

"Please don't argue with them, Dad," he says as we walk along the road in the full glare of local publicity. Neighbours stand by their gates to watch; there are no twitching curtains here. They miss nothing – one of the main advantages of long-term unemployment – and two visits in as many days suggest real trouble and any pretence at not being nosey is out the window and on the street. A couple who only last week had us all entertained as she screamed from an upstairs window to call the police, while her partner smashed the front room window in his efforts to break in and smash her skull – Barry from next door had to restrain him in the end – even these two are temporarily reunited to catch today's show. Sarah from upstairs is by our shared front gate; John is at work (presumably one of the reasons Sarah still puts up with him). There's no sign of Suzie. Tomas and I continue to walk.

"I think they're going to make trouble for us," I say to Tomas. He looks up at me and I explain. "Because they don't know what's happening with your Mum, then they're going to bother us so it looks like they're doing something." After this morning's visit from Social Services I know that anything is possible now, that we're in the silly season as they say in the soccer tabloids. This is no help to Tomas – none of this is bringing his Mum back home. "Don't be scared," I say to him but I realise immediately that he's not and I feel incredibly proud.

"Mr Isaacs," says the policewoman, "we'd like to ask you a few more questions." The two of them are waiting by the car rather than in the car as they did yesterday, presumably in case we decide to make a run for it.

"You'd best come inside, then," I say.

"Not here," says the filth, "down at the station."

"I can't do that," I say. "I'm not taking Tomas to a police station. Isn't it possible to talk here?"

"There's somebody wants to speak to you at head office," he says.

"And can't they come here?" I ask.

"Mr Isaacs," says the policewoman, "it really would be better if you come with us."

"Are you arresting me?" I ask.

"No," says the filth, "but we will if we have to."

"On suspicion of whatever you want, I guess."

"Something like that," he says.

"Mr Isaacs," she says, "this isn't up to us anymore; it really is best if you come along as we ask. Have you someone to mind your child?"

Trouble. Coming to my door. I'm not getting out of this and I look around. I know Caitlin is out there somewhere and I don't believe I will ever be able to forgive her for this. I don't even explain to Tomas what I need to do; I just take his hand and lead him to Suzie's gate. Her door is closed, uncommon enough in itself and I have to knock. There's no bell and no knocker and I realise I've never knocked before, always just called through an open door. There's no reply from inside so I knock again. Still no reply and I talk to the door,

"Suzie." There are no open windows but I know Suzie is home. "Suzie, it's Greg," I shout a little louder and then "please." Oh, this is a good show; we're putting on a good show here for y'all.

"I don't think she's in," says Tomas. Every moment

something new for Tomas – his Mum disappears; his Dad has to go with the police and now Suzie not at home? I'm about to shout again when the door opens.

"Suzie," I say, "I need you to – "

"I can't help you Greg," she says from behind the half-open door. "I can't get involved."

"Please Suzie," I say. "I just need you to mind Tomas for an hour or so. I have to go with them."

"What have you done?" she asks looking at me. In Suzie's world nothing is new, there is nothing I could have done that she's not come across before. Her question unnerves me.

"Nothing," I say. "I've done nothing. They just want to talk to me." Suzie continues to look at me before lowering her gaze to Tomas – him she can't refuse. She reaches out to gather him towards her, putting her arms around his shoulders. He's inside the house and the door is closed before I even have chance to say goodbye, so I shout it through the door.

"Tomas, I'll see you in a short while." My words sound hollow and again I'm conscious of the whole street watching my performance. I turn and face them and nod to the policewoman. Tomas will be fine with Suzie, this I know; he'll be fed and she loves him too much to let him come to any harm. What he must be thinking, I don't know and can't do anything about until I get him home. Once again, it's the effect on Tomas that strikes me as the worst of any given situation. Caitlin going missing is bad but Tomas losing his Mum is worse; Gregory being arrested is bad but leaving Tomas alone is worse.

The policewoman opens the rear door of the car and I get inside quietly.

"Things a bit different now, eh?" says the filth but I say nothing. I stare out the window. As we make our way into town against the early rush-hour traffic, it looks as though we really are going to head office. Yes, I have to agree, things are a little different now.

We pull up outside the large offices just off Piccadilly, functional and barely distinguishable from the dole office further down the street – no nostalgic or evocative visit to

Jackson's Row Police Station then. The filth stays in the car as his partner opens my door and escorts me inside, past the front desk and up the side stairway. I'm led into an open-plan office, which is very similar to how I imagine Caitlin's workplace, and then into a room with the sign Interview Room 1 on the door. Neither of us speaks a word until she asks me to sit down.

"I'll be back in one second," she says and leaves me alone in the room. There's a chair either side of a table, plastic and stackable. I take the seat with my back to the door, placing my jacket on the chair before I sit down. There's no natural light in the room but I already have a sense of winter darkness about to fall outside; the cold, bright spell of the past week is about to come to an end. I look at the clock on the wall – just before four-thirty. The policewoman comes back in and says,

"Detective Sand will be here in one minute. Before he arrives you might give me a few names, your partner's friends, people she may have contacted."

I give her Rosie and Bill.

"Caitlin stayed with them when she first came back to Manchester, soon after Tomas was born."

"Do you have a number for them?"

"Only back at the house." I tell her where they live. "I could phone it through to you tomorrow, if you like."

"We should be able to find them but yes, if you would." She reaches into a pocket for a card that she marks with her pen. "That's the number you should call."

"Maybe they'll be a bit more forthcoming with you," I say.

"Do you have reason to suspect they know something but won't tell you?" she asks.

"Short of something having happened to Caitlin, that seems to be the most obvious explanation."

"That she's staying with friends?"

"It would be the happiest outcome, I think, all things considered."

"And would these people really not tell you anything, at least that she was OK – provided of course that Caitlin has gone to them?"

"They'd do whatever Caitlin asked them to do," I say.

"And that seems unlikely, that she wouldn't at least put her son's mind at rest?"

"Yes," I agree.

"And are there other friends she may have contacted?"

"Only people from work and you know where to get in touch with them." I list off the names most likely.

"No one else?"

"If there is, then I don't know about them."

"You mean she could be with another man?"

I shrug.

"Anything's possible," I say.

"But you prefer to believe otherwise?"

"Naturally."

For a second I pick up at least a hint of sympathy – or is it pity? The policewoman then straightens, almost to attention, as a heavyset man in a suit walks briskly into the room.

"Mr Isaacs," he says shaking my hand, "my name is Detective John Sand. Thank you for coming in to see me." Like I had a choice. "I need to ask you a few questions about the disappearance of Ms Caitlin O'Connor. PC Byrne here will stay to take notes but this is not an official interview as such. You're not under arrest and are free to go if you don't feel inclined to answer my questions. Is this acceptable to you?"

He's all business, brusque but affable. He can afford to be – he knows I'm in no position to refuse. This is probably the point where I should ask for legal advice or representation but I've no experience in this. There's a grey area here between my rights and how the police will construe my actions.

"Mr Isaacs?" I still take a second to answer.

"Whatever will help you find Caitlin," I say.

"Good," he says satisfied, "that's exactly my interest in this matter."

"Why?" I ask.

"Sorry?" he says.

"Why are you so interested in finding Caitlin? How many missing persons have been reported in Manchester this week? I know for a fact that you don't show this much interest in them all."

"That's a fair comment," he says, "but humour me, would you? I'm interested in the circumstances of Ms O'Connor's disappearance, how it's connected to the trouble at her workplace. I agree I'd never have come across the fact that she'd gone missing if there hadn't been the riot at Rusholme Social Security Office but now I have and here we are. More to the point, Mr Isaacs, I would like to ask you why you're not more interested in Ms O'Connor's disappearance."

I don't answer for a while and then say,

"Riot?"

"Whatever," he says dismissively and again there's a silence between us.

"What would you have me do?" I ask.

"Well," he says, "show a little more concern for a start but on a more practical front, there a several things you could have been doing this past week."

"Such as?"

"Checking with the hospitals for one –," he says.

"You see, that's where it begins," I interrupt.

"Where what begins?" he asks.

"Your ignorance, your PC Plodding about the place. The fact that I asked a friend of mine to check the hospitals wouldn't occur to you, would it? And because it doesn't occur to you then you think maybe it means something. What else could I have been doing? Please, I wish I knew but hearing it come from you is rich, given the police record on missing persons."

"And your friend came up with nothing through the hospitals?"

"No."

"But there," he says, "We have a start, you see. Here I was, worried about your lack of concern and now you put my mind at rest. Already we have some progress, yes?" I say nothing. "Yes?" he repeats.

"If you want to talk about lack of concern, then maybe they should have been taking notes when I reported her missing at

Parrs Wood station. Or maybe PC Byrne's colleague could fill us in on his lack of concern?" Detective Sand looks behind me to PC Byrne and then down to the notes in front of him.

"You don't think much of us then, no?" Inviting me to talk when I know I've already said too much. "No possibility that at least some of us may have your best interests at heart?"

"Please," I say.

"No, come on. Feel free to speak." I don't – speak that is, or feel free to do so. He lets it go and returns to his notes. He really does appear to be reading them and then sits for a full minute studying me. A minute is a long time for silence but I know the tactic and I look blankly at the table. "Not the most forthcoming person in the world, are you?" he asks. I look at him and say,

"Ask me a specific question that is relevant to why I'm here."

"OK," he says, "here goes – you were arrested several years ago for fighting in the centre of town. Does your – what shall we call it – your antipathy towards the police stem from that incident?"

"Relevant?" I say.

"I think so, yes," he says. "I really do want to understand what is going on here."

"Then I would say partly."

"Only partly? How do you view that incident? Can you remember?"

"Myself and some friends were waiting for a late night bus in Piccadilly. We had different accents to some other people at the bus stop and they started beating us up for that reason alone. The police came and arrested me. I lost my glasses in the fight and couldn't see."

"You're not from Manchester originally then, no? No, let me guess," he says holding up his hand. "Yorkshire somewhere, but not Leeds, I think."

"York," I say.

"Ah York," he says, "beautiful city. And you presumably moved here when you came to college?"

"Yes."

"You don't wear glasses now?"

"Contacts," I say.

"And how do you find them? I only ask because my wife is thinking of trying this new laser treatment and it worries me. I'd much rather she tried contacts but she can't stand the thought of them. You'd think she – " but he's lost me again and stops. "Why only partly to blame – you're not denying you're not exactly our biggest fan?"

"Ask your colleagues at Orgreave," I say.

"Oh, come on," he says laughing. "You're not serious about that, surely?" He waits but gets no reply. "You know that photograph was made up, don't you?"

"No," I say, "I know that photograph wasn't made up and don't see much to laugh about there."

It takes something like Orgreave – a photograph of a mounted policeman about to baton a woman on the head – for most people to question the police. For me, it just confirms what I already know.

"But no," says Sand, as though dismissing the whole argument, "give me something a little closer to home, something relevant as you might say."

"OK then, why did I receive a visit from the Social Services this morning?"

"Ah," he says and again looks behind me. "PC Byrne's colleague maybe being a little too, er, over-eager shall we say?"

"The guy's a scumbag in a uniform."

"Oh now," says Sand, "that's a little harsh, don't you think?"

"No? Tell me – I'm thinking of applying, what qualifications do I need to join? Two O'Levels, good eyesight and to be over a certain height – oh, and to be a complete and utter moron." Saying too much, Gregory.

"Well," he says smiling, "that clears that up." But I'm on a roll now and can't stop.

"Coppers like him are just filth," I say, "and nothing will ever change my opinion of them."

"I think I have the picture now," says Sand smiling. "Shall

we move on? How long have you known Ms O'Connor?"

"A couple of years," I say.

"And when you met her she was already resident at your current address?"

"Yes, well, she was just about to move in."

"And her son, Tomas, he's what age? Five?"

"Yes, nearly six."

"He regards you as his Dad, is that right? But he's old enough to know you're not his real father?"

"That's right," I say.

"How does that work for you? I mean, are you OK with that?"

"It works for us all."

"But it's happened very quickly, wouldn't you say? There you are, one day a young single man with little or no responsibilities and then the next minute – bang! The full works, no?"

"A little like getting somebody pregnant," I say and immediately regret it when Sand looks up. "I mean – people's lives do change quickly once children are involved."

"But it suits you, you seem to have adapted quite well."

"Yes."

"Your work, Mr Isaacs – "

"Oh Christ, here we go," I say. "I'm trying to be a writer, OK?"

"Ye-es," he says broadly and emphatically, "absolutely OK with me – that's why I asked you about it. Fascinating, tell me – what kind of stuff do you write? I've fancied it myself before now but well, you know, unlikely ever to get round to it. Go on."

"Go on, what?"

"Tell all."

"You're taking the piss," I say.

"I most assuredly am not," he says. "If you don't wish to discuss it, fine, I understand but the money, Mr Isaacs, I need to know about the money you make."

"So you can see if I'm fiddling the dole?"

"No," he says, "was that the impression you picked up

yesterday? No, I just need to understand how your home life works, to get a full picture, you see. I don't think there's anything improper happening here; I simply wish to understand."

"And this will help you find Caitlin?"

"Maybe, we're both in the dark here. Anything could help."

"I make very little beyond what I'm given by the government and the occasional typing job I manage to pick up."

"And again, you're OK with this? Worth the struggle and all that?"

"No, I wish I earned a fortune from my writing but I can't see that happening just yet."

"And Caitlin – Ms O'Connor? How do you say her name? I hate saying Ms all the time but I don't want to offend you by saying her name wrong."

"Whatever you're comfortable with is fine," I say. "What about her?"

"She's OK with you bringing so little into the home, financially, I mean?"

"Everything seems to suit us both fine for the moment," I say.

"Yes," he agrees, "but then we have this problem, don't we, of her disappearing and then obviously something isn't quite so all right. Do you agree?"

"Yes."

"Good," he says, "so let's move on to this then, yes?"

"Yes, let's."

Sand takes a moment to reflect. He's different; I'll give him that – a thinking man's copper.

"On Monday Caitlin had what anybody would describe as a bad day at the office," he says. He looks up but I'm trying only to speak when he asks me a direct question. I can't resist though.

"Tuesday would have been worse," I say.

"Yes, yes," he agrees. "We'll come on to Tuesday in a second but for now, Monday – a bad day?"

"Yes."

"Made worse perhaps by it being her first day back after a period of sick leave?"

"I guess, yes."

"And I guess," he says, "that maybe she wasn't quite ready to return to work, it all became too much for her and then – then we don't know what, do we?" I don't reply. "Is that pretty much your reading of the situation?" he asks.

"Yes," I say.

"It doesn't give us much, does it? Not a lot there to go on?"

"What happened to your 'Caitlin instigating a riot' theory?"

"Our what?"

"You know, the Burkes were Irish, Caitlin's Irish; therefore she must have encouraged them to come in the next day and trash the gaff. Good reason for not turning into work. What's happened to them, by the way, the Burke family?"

"Oh they're back where they belong," he says. "Let the Irish look after their own is what I say, at least where they're concerned. Don't tell me, your sympathy goes out to them?"

"I would imagine that Caitlin's did," I say.

"Yes, I believe so too, to the extent of trying to help them as much as her job allowed. The impression I have of your partner is of someone who actually tries to act on her convictions." I ignore the inference that I, on the other hand…

"And you think she may have gone too far this time?" I ask.

"Oh no," he says, "not at all. No, from what I can make out Caitlin O'Connor acted absolutely professionally in this case, as she seems to have done in all matters of her workplace. From my enquiries into what happened on Tuesday morning then Ms O'Connor is about the only person to come out this whole debacle blame-free." He leans forward, close to my face. "Hence my concern."

"That's a little different to your colleagues' reaction yesterday."

"Well, give me some credit here Mr Isaacs. Yes, it was the usual story of incompetence and blame, like any workplace really. The only reason we became involved – I became involved – is the Burke family being so…" – he searches for the word – "…violent, really. Yes, threateningly violent, to the extent of causing personal injury, so in come the police."

I smile.

"Mr Isaacs?"

"Let me guess – Harry Horwich – they singled him out?"

Sand smiles too now and nods his head in admiration.

"Very good, Mr Isaacs, very good. Although really, if anyone is to blame for Tuesday then it's Mr Horwich himself. Talk about incompetence. I can't say he managed the situation too well. Could maybe have been a little more sympathetic, if you know what I mean, understood what the Burkes were going through."

"No doubt he had Caitlin in his face at the time."

"Yes, I suspect so, but really, everybody knows there's a time to follow rules and a time to stretch them. As far as Mr Horwich was concerned his Department had done all they were obliged to do and that was an end to the matter. Of course, on paper he's right but you would hope for a little more initiative in your senior managers."

"But the end result is still the same?"

"I suppose so. We thought it best in the end, for everybody involved that is, to just let the whole thing drop. Best to just move on."

"Except for the Burkes," I say.

"Yes, except for the Burkes," Sand agrees, "but I can't really help them now."

"And Caitlin, of course."

"Yes, Caitlin. You've followed my line of reasoning perfectly – once the matter was settled then I couldn't help but worry about Caitlin O'Connor. I presumed at first she must have gone back on the sick list but then I hear she's missing and I start to worry. So no, we don't give each missing person this amount of attention but I would have thought you might have been appreciative rather than…." Again, looking for the right word. "What are you being, Mr Isaacs? Uncooperative?"

"Pardon me if you're the one good copper that proves to be the exception," I say.

"You've really got it bad, haven't you?" he asks. "Let's get over all that though and concentrate on the matter in hand –

do you know of any reason why Ms O'Connor may have gone missing after work on Monday evening?"

"Yes," I say, "lots of reasons but none of them seem sufficient for her still to be missing."

"Well let's start with one, shall we? You've said you think she was upset? Both of us agree that maybe she wasn't fit for work but do you really think that what happened to the Burkes was enough to – unhinge her?"

"She takes things very personally."

"A tough job to be in then? Especially on that front counter?"

"I couldn't agree more."

"And you've said as much to Ms O'Connor in the past?"

"We've talked about it but I'm not in a position to tell her what to do."

"No, but you'd rather she were more a paperwork type of person?"

"She wouldn't be Caitlin then. I think she believes that if it wasn't her on the front counter then it may be the likes of Harry Horwich; there's enough of them about."

"What do you think most upset her about the Burkes' case?"

"We don't know for certain that she was upset, do we?"

"No, but I think we can both guess. What would it be – the fact they were Irish? That they were to move in around the corner from you? Or would it be the sheer vindictiveness, so it seemed, of her Department? Having to put up with the likes of Harry Horwich when her heart went out to these people? What would it have been?"

"I don't know."

"But hazard a guess, from what you know of Caitlin."

"I would say it was all those things but mainly it would be the personal misfortune of such a thing happening to a family."

"And of course, it happening so close to home, on her own street in fact. It doesn't say much for the people living there, does it?"

I refuse to be drawn on this.

"If they had children," I say, "then that's what would have freaked Caitlin out."

"Oh they had children alright, no end of children."

"But I still don't believe that alone would keep her away from home all this time."

"No," he agrees, "and yet you don't feel able to explain why she would be further upset by things at home. We all get sick Mr Isaacs and sometimes we become upset, but not to the extent of disappearing."

"We've had some very upsetting news and Caitlin was just getting over it."

"But you can't or won't tell me what this news was about?"

"No, it's very personal and very upsetting, particularly for Caitlin. Can you accept that for now?"

"Yes, I can respect that but I do need to keep asking questions, PC Plodding around the place, as you might say, so please, don't be offended by anything I ask. OK?"

"OK."

"How were you and Ms O'Connor getting along – how were you both coping with your upsetting news?"

"It was tough enough but I thought we were pulling through, especially after meeting her on Monday lunchtime. She seemed a lot more like herself."

"Had you rowed recently, sufficiently to make her feel like not coming home?"

"No," I say, "there was more crying than rowing."

"Now I have to ask you this, Mr Isaacs, so please don't get angry. Could she just have left you, had enough and gone away for good?"

"Me, yes," I say, "but she'd never leave Tomas, her son. That doesn't make any sense."

"What if she'd really had enough, including Tomas? What if whatever was upsetting her had just tipped the whole lot over and she walked away from everything?"

"I don't believe she could do that.".

"But we don't think rationally at these times, Mr Isaacs, and even if she had thought it through, she knows you're there to look after Tomas. Maybe she really did just call time out?"

"I don't believe she could," I repeat.

"Do you ever hit her, Mr Isaacs?"

"Hit Caitlin?"

"Yes, when arguments become too much, that sort of thing. Please don't take offence but it is something I have to ask."

"No," I say, "I don't hit her."

"Have you ever?"

"No." He doesn't speak, again presumably trying the 'if I stay quiet then maybe he'll talk' approach.

"You wouldn't be unusual if you did," he says after a while. "It's a sorry state of affairs I know but I think it's more common than not."

Again the silence; this time he even stands up out of his chair, walks to the corner of the room and looks at a blank TV monitor bracketed to the wall. When I look up, I can see him watching my reflection in the screen. He has his hands on his hips and as he turns around his stance accentuates the paunch of his belly, his white shirt straining around his waist.

"You're having a rough time," he says and at first I believe he's referring to this interview but he continues. "You've had some bad news and you're trying really hard to come through it together. But nothing you do seems to be enough, does it? Just when you think you're getting through to her, she goes off the rails again and you're back to square one. It's exasperating – you love her but she's really trying your patience. And then one night, for some reason, any reason or no reason, when you feel you're unable to reason, you resort to your fist or your open hand in an attempt to get it into her thick skull. A second only, an absolutely temporary moment but there, it's done and although you immediately regret it, you also feel better because now, maybe now, she's going to come to her senses? Have you never gone through that in your head, Mr Isaacs?"

His question is so pertinent to Caitlin that it unnerves me. I think it was John's violence against Sarah on Sunday night that did for any chance of Caitlin recovering from our trip to the hospital. He's wrong about me though.

"Have you even just thought about it?" he continues. "I know I have – sometimes I could, oh, I don't know, sometimes when you talk and talk and still don't get through, it's tough, you know?" This last he actually says to PC Byrne.

"I've never hit Caitlin," I say.

"And you believe you never could?" He's straight back at me.

"I believe I never could but I know enough of the world to understand it's always a possibility."

"And if it's always a possibility in our minds," he says, "imagine how it is in theirs?" Again, he gestures towards PC Byrne as the only female in the room. "Have you ever hit a woman?" he asks.

"No," I say.

"Never?" he asks and sits down to return to his notes. As soon as he does so, I know where he's going with it.

"That's bullshit!"

"But there was a woman at the scene and she was prepared to make a statement to the effect that you attacked her."

"That's police bullshit and you know it. Of course she was prepared to make a statement – it got her own friends off the hook and it got me convicted. They started the fight and then the police came along and finished it."

"That night still rankles, doesn't it?"

"I don't go out much in town anymore, if that's what you mean?" I say.

"Do you go out much at all?" he asks. "I mean, you've no workplace to go to and you've to be there all the time for your son, or your partner's son. I'm wondering – how much interaction do you actually have with the world?"

I don't reply and he lets it drop. "No matter," he says. "You say you were just getting to know Ms O'Connor when she moved into what is now your home?"

"Yes."

"But you weren't an item as yet, you weren't 'going' with each other?"

"We'd just started seeing each other."

"Yet Ms O'Connor was allocated the property on the strength of her being a single parent?"

"She was a single parent."

"And she was allocated the property on the strength of that?" he repeats.

"Yes."

"You hadn't started your own parenting at this stage, then?"

"I'd just started seeing her."

"But I'd say you put a lot of effort into the property? By all accounts you have it set up pretty well."

"It needed it."

"And you would work on the flat while Ms O'Connor was at work?"

"Some days, yes."

"But it wasn't at this stage what you considered to be your family home?"

"I still had my own place to live."

"But you would sometimes stay over?"

"Yes," I say, "it happens."

"Naturally," says Sand, "naturally. And during this time, what were you thinking? What were your plans?"

"Sorry?"

"You know, what did you aim to get out of the situation?"

"I was hoping to get laid," I say, "which I was."

"Excellent!" says Sand. "What else?"

"I was falling in love with Caitlin and at the same time with Tomas."

"And eventually you all agreed it was best that you move in and live together as a family?"

"Yes."

"Excellent," says Sand again. "You see, I have my picture now of you and your family and how you work together. My colleague PC Byrne here has already told me how well you seem suited to your role as Tomas's dad and now I can see that it's true. What we need to do now is work our way on from here to figure out what may have become of Ms O'Connor."

"Yes," I agree.

"Yes," he says, "yes, yes, yes," and then nothing. He makes to stand and then decides against it. He replaces all his notes in a cardboard folder and pushes them to one side of the table. "There's a big hole in my understanding…" he begins but doesn't continue. He looks across the table directly into my eyes. I hold his stare for a moment but then look down again. "There's something very wrong here, Mr Isaacs, something very wrong. I fear for Ms O'Connor's safety."

"Yes."

"Yes," he repeats. "But what I think I fear, Mr Isaacs, is you. I'm glad you agreed to come here today because it's made me see what's missing here. You see, I think at the very heart of this – what's wrong here – is you. I can't think of any other explanation and now that I've met you then I see what everyone else can see. I think I agree with my colleagues on this one. You may not like us very much Mr Isaacs, Mr Gregory Isaacs, but it's nothing compared to how I feel about you. I think you're a bit of a cold fish, if you don't mind my saying and I don't know what you've done, or what you think you're doing, but I will find out."

I look away and shake my head.

"And you can come on all world-weary, here we go again, and so on and so on, but this time I think you've done something very wrong indeed and I intend to find out what it is."

I close my eyes as though this will prevent me from hearing this bullshit.

"What I don't understand," he says, "is what you hope to achieve. You see – your name isn't on the tenancy agreement so you don't get the flat. You don't have any rights over Tomas, so the Social Services will indeed be calling and the boy will more than likely end up in care, or worse, with his real father. And we know you can't have any more children – " I look up. "Oh yes, we know all about that," he says. "We know that's your upsetting news – the news you haven't even got the balls to tell us. So, what do you hope to get out of all this? You've fucked up the one chance you had of any sort of a decent life with Caitlin, so what's left? No," he says, "I think you've done

something…" He does his searching for the word thing again –
"…something regrettable. And I intend to find out just what."

"What would you have me do?" I ask.

"I don't much care," he says. "I believe you reported her as
missing yesterday as a cynical exercise to be seen to be doing
something at least, so I don't much care what you do now. You
carry on playing at being Tomas's dad while I try to find out
what has happened to Ms O'Connor."

"Am I free to go?"

"Yes, yes, off you go," he says in his dismissive way. "I shall
call you if I need you."

So I pick up my jacket and leave. I walk past PC Byrne – who
fails to look me in the eye – and then out into the featureless
office, where I notice there are fewer people than when I first
arrived. I check the time on my watch – almost six o'clock. I
cross the office floor to the stairway and then go down to the
reception area. Even here it's quiet and this adds to the unreality
of the situation. Outside it's dark and the weather has indeed
changed – a strong gust is blowing down from Piccadilly and
the sky is heavy with snow. No police car waits by the entrance
to take me home so I head into the wind. I have money for the
bus but I'm not dressed for the weather and it's bitterly cold as
I walk. At this rate it will be at least seven before I arrive home
and I pray that Tomas is OK and not too worried.

Same old, same old, I think about the filth – they're all filth
when you get right down to it – but I do have a sense that if
Caitlin doesn't come home soon then Sand could make some
serious trouble for me. I stand and wait in Piccadilly. I've just
missed a bus. I have plenty of time to go over what was said
and where it leaves me now.

Had Sand already made up his mind about me before I
went in? Was I wrong about that policewoman when I sensed
she at least felt something for what I'm going through? My
thoughts turn to Caitlin. What if she is staying with a friend
and has asked them not to say? Is it worth phoning around
again? What if she's with someone else – as in, with Someone
Else? But it seems more and more likely to me that something

has happened to her – an accident or something, I don't know – and the mystery will only be resolved once this accident becomes known.

There's something else I think about too, as the bus arrives and I make my way home – did I do anything, even without realising it, that caused Caitlin to go missing?

When he hit her it came from nowhere.

Caitlin went over it later, again and again, and could only think that maybe it was as she undressed. She took her clothes off unconsciously and unselfconsciously in front of Immy as though this were a night like any other. Tiredness was taking her over, a profound weariness that after the restaurant was almost a pleasure to give in to. They'd achieved so much together throughout evening; part of that achievement was to know what to avoid and what to ignore. Perhaps she'd been wrong to ask about the business? Caitlin knew they were both still treading carefully; maybe she should have gone to the bathroom to get undressed and been more aware of the effect her nakedness would have on Immy. She felt so big and lumpy it never even occurred to her.

Imran left the room as she was undressing; she put on a nightshirt, large enough to be comfortable and in no way sexually suggestive. Maybe it was her plainness, her ugliness being laid bare? What had she done to make him change so?

When Imran came back into the bedroom, he walked over to where Caitlin sat on the edge of the bed and when she looked up he swung the back of his fist up against the side of her mouth. The impact knocked her back and to the side, though she put out her arm to prevent herself falling back fully on to the bed. He moved his foot between her legs and from this better vantage point thumped hard down on to her cheek and nose. She crumpled to a heap.

"If you ever try that again then I'll fucking kill you," he said. So it was coming all along, she might have known. There was no way he could have let her get away with it; no way could he forgive her trying to leave. She had it coming. "Do you hear me?"

Caitlin could hear Imran but the blow had dislodged something in her head – was it blood? She nodded her head, or rather, let her head drop to her chin.

"Do you hear me?" shouted Imran.

"Yes," she said quietly.

"What the fuck did you think you were up to?"

Caitlin realised he was waiting for a reply.

"I don't know," she said. A wave of pain surged through her and she instinctively covered her belly and closed her eyes.

"Where were you going to go?"

"I don't know," she said. "Manchester." He was still standing above her with one foot positioned between her legs, pushing her right leg against the bed. Her nightshirt had ridden up and Caitlin felt exposed but didn't dare to adjust her clothing. She still held on to her belly. She opened her eyes but looked down towards the bed, only seeing Imran at the edge of her vision. When he spoke again, he did so in a quieter voice that was no less threatening for all that.

"Nobody wants you there," he said. "You belong here now, you belong to me. Did you think I would just let you go?"

"No," said Caitlin. "I know, I'm sorry."

He relaxed his leg away from her own and she became conscious for the first time of, Imran's breathing; short, sharp intakes of breath, almost like a sob. She didn't know this man, she never knew this man that Imran became. Had he always been there and it was just that she had never seen? Whatever, this was not the man she thought she'd known. She must have somehow changed him, brought this upon herself, but how? And why?

Imran stayed in the same position for some time and Caitlin hoped this might mean an end to it. She could feel Imran looking at her but she didn't dare look back. In the past his shame had made him worse before it became any safer.

"Lift up your nightshirt," he said after a while.

Caitlin said nothing but began to cry.

"Lift up your nightshirt, I said."

"Please don't hurt the baby, Immy, please," she pleaded.

"Lift up your nightshirt."

Slowly Caitlin relaxed her arms from around her belly and pulled the material towards her chin. She was weeping openly now, begging please but almost resigned to whatever might happen. Imran looked down at her, his face a mixture of lust and loathing. From his back pocket he pulled out a knife and the sound of it opening caused Caitlin to recoil in horror.

"Oh God, no."

"Open your legs."

"For God's sake, Immy, please."

"Open your legs and your baby will be safe. Anything else from you and I'll kill you both."

Later – and there would be a later, there would be something after this, there would be a tomorrow and her life would go on – she would question how she'd managed to turn on to her back and open her legs to Immy. But by then she knew the answer was that she would do anything to save her baby and also that this baby was going to give her the strength to get through this and then away. If it had gone on then she would have gone on, whatever it took to save her baby.

Imran brought the blade close to between Caitlin's legs. She felt him press the point of the knife against her and she let out a sound, an anguished noise from deep inside.

"Shut up!" he said, pressing harder. "This," he said with a further push, "this belongs to me. You belong to me and I can do to you whatever I choose to do. Your baby belongs to me and whether he lives or dies is up to me. Do you understand?"

Caitlin tried to speak but no words came.

"Do you understand?" he shouted.

Surely somebody could hear him? Surely somebody could hear?

"Yes," she said.

"So if you ever try a stunt like that again then you know what will happen, don't you?"

"Yes," she said.

"Good," said Imran and with a little flick of the knife he cut her before walking away.

Seven

It's later than seven and dark as I knock on Suzie's open front door. It's bitterly cold. Tomas jumps up and runs across the crowded room – Suzie, Barry and Olivia are all at home as well as two young lads of about fifteen – and he hugs me around the waist. I lean down and kiss his cheek, putting my arms around his shoulders. What must he have been going through, first with Caitlin disappearing and then me being taken off by the police? No amount of reassuring hugs could ever make up for the past few hours. Caitlin always tells me that kids are resilient but surely this is pushing it? And what has Suzie been telling him? That he should hope for the best or that he should fear for the worst?

The two teenagers pick up a pile of videocassettes and say their goodbyes to Suzie.

"Thanks for these," says one of them.

"Thanks, Suzie," I echo after they've left.

"We need to talk," says Suzie. "You had some Pakis call earlier – what was that about?" She shows no awareness of Tomas being here – Tomas is Tomas and Pakis are Pakis.

Barry leans across from his armchair and reaches over to the coffee table for a packet of cigarettes, a huge physical presence in such a small crowded room. He takes his lead from Suzie and is none too welcoming. I'm struck once again by the fact that without Caitlin my being here makes no sense whatsoever. If I'm good enough for Caitlin then I'm good enough for Suzie and her family but take away Caitlin and I just don't belong.

To her credit, Olivia lightens the tone by suggesting she takes Tomas home to get ready for bed. Tomas is initially reluctant – having thought he had me back he doesn't now want to let me go – but because it's Olivia then he's persuaded.

"Five minutes," I say to him, handing the keys to Olivia.

Tomas has his coat on from sitting in Suzie's front room. Even in this weather the front door is left open to the elements.

"Come on," says Olivia, "it's not every young man I ask to show me his bedroom."

"Olivia," he says, trying to make out that he's embarrassed when really he's pleased at the attention, and I can see that he's OK.

"Can I sit down?" I ask Suzie and she nods to a chair.

"So then," she says, "let's have it. The Pakis first."

For all that's happened, it's this that's eating her most; that some Pakistanis should come onto the estate. I wouldn't mind but she has people of every race, colour and creed visit her, both for business and for sex. Or maybe it's simply that this is the most recent of the unexplained events I've brought to the estate these past few days.

"They weren't just any Pakis either," says Barry.

I don't know what he means by this so I address myself to Suzie.

"My guess is that Tomas's father has found out where we live. I think Social Services have told him that Caitlin's missing."

"And he's crawled out the woodwork to make trouble for Tomas?" says Suzie.

"Something like that," I say. "I think he's a – a bad sort." It seems pretty lame compared to how I feel about Imran, if it was Imran that called.

"You're not kidding," says Barry. "Do you know who he is, what he does?"

"What do you mean?"

"Well, I don't know if this was the same guy but I do know that the person knocking for you earlier is into some very bad stuff indeed. Not a nice man."

"Did you speak to him?"

Suzie answers.

"When we heard someone call then we went out to check. We thought it could have been something to do with Caitlin."

"Did Tomas see who it was?"

"No, he's been kept occupied by Olivia all evening. Would

he know his father to see him?"

"No, he's never met him. What did this guy say?"

"Nothing much," says Barry. "Just asked if anyone was home. If it wasn't Tomas's father then you don't want this person calling to your home."

"I don't want him calling whoever he is," I say.

"Wasn't there a barring order put on him?" asks Suzie.

"Yes, I pointed that out to Social Services this morning, but the order's to keep him away from Caitlin, not from Tomas."

"And where's Caitlin, Gregory? What's happened to her?"

"I don't know Suzie, I really don't know." There's a part of me that objects to being answerable to Suzie, that resents having to justify myself to her or the police or Social Services, especially when I'm as much in the dark as they are. I still can't figure out if Suzie is being a good friend or an interfering neighbour, whether it's self-interest or selfless concern. I believe she would do anything for Tomas or Caitlin but I don't think she really trusts me; or likes me even, come to think of it. I go over the past few days for Suzie's benefit, specifically Caitlin returning to work on Monday and then not coming home. I start to explain about the family at number five being burnt out and the likely effect this would have had on Caitlin at work but I can see I'm getting nowhere.

"But she wasn't in work on Tuesday when it all went off," says Suzie as though this and not a family losing their home is the issue.

"I think it was too much for Caitlin to handle on her first day back," I say. "Or at least, that was what I thought. I'm not too sure now."

"What do you mean?"

"Well, when Caitlin didn't come home at first then I thought it must be everything getting on top of her. You know, she's been off sick; we've had some bad news and then being handed that case when she went back to work. I was finding it hard too and perhaps I wasn't as sympathetic as I might have been. I presumed Caitlin had gone to stay with a friend to, you know, get away for a while."

"And now?"

"Now, I don't know. I think she's been gone too long. Whatever about me, I know she couldn't live without Tomas. I'm afraid that something has happened to her."

"And what about the police, what do they think?"

"They think her disappearance is suspicious." Suzie looks at me. "They think they have reason to be suspicious of me."

"And do they?" she asks.

I take my time before answering, partly because my first instinct is to say 'Fuck you!' But I don't, for Tomas' sake.

"I believe the only thing I'm guilty of is not caring enough for Caitlin. Maybe if I'd been there for her she would have been OK." I don't add that I was also at the end of my tether – I'm not going to win over any friends here this evening.

"And what do you think might have happened?" asks Suzie.

"An accident maybe, or that she's done something stupid to herself."

"Things were that bad?" she asks.

Again I take my time.

"Things were bad but I didn't think they were that bad. But the longer she stays away … now I don't know what to think."

"We've heard nothing, have we Barry?"

Barry shakes his head in agreement. Whatever they think of me, they do care for Caitlin and they do have a large enough network of connections to at least have heard something. If Caitlin's staying with friends then she's either not going out or not in the area.

"You'd best get round to Tomas," says Suzie.

"Yes," I say.

"And Gregory?"

"Yes?"

"I meant what I said about the filth. I can't have them calling around here, it's too close to home." I nod. "Sort it out," she adds.

Interview over.

I can see that Olivia would like to stay and the idea appeals to me. More than appeals to me. I don't know where this is coming from – sympathy, a crush I never knew she had – but whatever it is there's no mistaking what she's about here. Girls always decide and we never have a clue how. She's ridiculously young, I'm not sure if she's even sixteen yet, but the idea of just losing myself in a kiss, who knows, maybe more – it would be nice. A kiss or a comfort fuck; I wouldn't mind anything to take my mind away from how useless I feel just waiting for Caitlin.

Olivia, true to her word, has Tomas ready for bed. He's in his pyjamas and the three of us stand in the living room. Olivia obviously has no intention of leaving but this is a pretty odd situation. Tomas is way too sharp not to notice.

"I have to get Tomas into bed," I explain. I know I need time alone with him after all that's happened today, time to reassure him that we're still in this together. I'm obviously not going to get that with Olivia still in the flat but she sits down, apparently intent on waiting and I don't feel much like sending her home.

It's early, close to eight o'clock, and I think I might have trouble getting Tomas to bed. But when I agree that he can sleep with me again then he goes to bed willingly. He says goodnight to Olivia, who stretches up from the sofa to kiss him on the cheek. I take him through to the bedroom and once we're alone then Tomas can't wait to ask what's most on his mind.

"Is Olivia staying?"

"Sshh," I say. "I'm going through to say goodbye to her, that's all, and thank her for looking after you. You're a nightmare," I add smiling.

"What?" he asks, all innocence. As he settles into the bed he says, "What did the police want?"

"Just to talk," I say. I look down at him and I know this won't do. "How about this?" I say. "I'll say goodbye to Olivia and then I'll come through to talk. We'll have some supper together in bed, if you like." I realise I'm starving; Tomas has eaten with Suzie but it would be a nice way to end an otherwise fairly shitty day.

"I didn't think you were going to come back," Tomas says. "Suzie said they might keep you in all night."

"No, it wasn't anything like that." Oh no? "Besides, even if I'd been really late, you know Suzie would look after you."

"Yes, I know, but…" It's not the same when first your Mum and then your Dad go missing – he has a point.

"Give me five minutes," I say, "and I'll be in. Would you like me to peel you an apple?"

"Yes please, and some juice."

Olivia follows me through to the kitchen. Given my lack of success at the supermarket this afternoon, there's not a whole lot in to eat. There's enough cheese and some bread to make a sandwich. I slice a tomato in an attempt to liven it up a little; it's not much but I'm so hungry that anything will do. I put on the kettle and I know I could quite easily take Tomas his apple and juice, eat my sandwich and enjoy a cup of tea here in the kitchen with Olivia; see what might happen. But I can't.

"Olivia, I have to go through to Tomas. I have to make sure he's OK."

"Yes, of course," she says jumping up. "I was just waiting to see that you were, you know, if you needed to talk or anything."

"I'm fine," I say, "really. And thanks." I reach to take her hand but she can't leave quickly enough. She smiles but it's not enough to cover her embarrassment. I see her to the door and she's gone.

Shit, shit, shit! So much for that!

I return to the kitchen, pick up the knife I'd used to slice the tomato, rinse it and peel an apple for Tomas. I make the tea, pour Tomas some juice and carry it all through on a tray. Tomas is sat up waiting and smiles as I sit down beside him on the bed. Resilience doesn't even begin to cover it.

"I spoke to the man who's in charge of looking for your Mum," I tell Tomas.

"The policeman?"

"Yes."

"Not the same one as yesterday, the one who came to collect you again today?"

"No, son, the man I saw today is the man in charge."

"Is he nicer?"

"Yes." And more intelligent, I want to say.

"What does he think?"

"He's as confused as we are. I also gave them the names of everyone we think might know something."

"Including Rosie and Bill?"

"Yes, only I have to phone the policewoman again tomorrow to give her the number."

"I was thinking," he says.

"Yes son?"

"Well, if I was in trouble or if I needed help or something, then I'd go to you or my Mum."

"Yes?"

"So, do you think that's where she's gone?"

"To her Mum and Dad? No, I don't think so; you know your Mum hasn't seen them for a long time."

"But maybe?"

"It's unlikely son, really." He gives me his look. "I'll tell you what – when I phone the policewoman with Rosie and Bill's number, then I'll tell her they should check into it. How about that?"

He's so trusting. I'm almost tempted to tell him I've begun to fear the worst but then I stop myself. No good would come from it and Tomas' hope and optimism are all he has – that and me. It's probably best that I don't tell him the police suspect me of doing his mother in. I wonder if the time will come when I have to sit him down and finally break his heart? It doesn't bear thinking about. I guess it all depends on what the police come up with and surely they'll find something soon?

I hold Tomas' hand in a feeble effort to reassure him but his hands are all sticky from the apple. At least it breaks the moment and we laugh together.

"Wait here," I say, "and I'll fetch you a cloth." As I return from the bathroom, there's a knock at the door. I hand the cloth to Tomas.

"Here," I say, "wipe around your mouth as well. It's time to settle down to sleep now. I'll be back in a moment to kiss you good night."

"Who's that going to be?" he asks.

"Well I don't know," I say smiling. But I think I do; I think it's Olivia and I close the bedroom door behind me.

But it's not Olivia; it's Imran, or at least someone I presume to be Imran. He looks older than I would have thought, with grey stubble across his chin, though still with a full head of jet-black hair. And smaller, even taking into account the front door step he's much shorter than I am. I don't know what I was expecting but this wasn't it. If anything, I think I hoped this day would never come – but it has. He doesn't speak, just stands there in the light from the hallway and slightly raises his head in acknowledgement. Beyond him, I can see two others waiting for him in the street.

"Yes?" I say.

He smiles, well, kind of stretches his upper lip.

"I think we both know what I want."

I do but I'll be damned if I'm going to make this easy for him.

"I want to see my son," he says. I'm immediately conscious of Tomas listening in the bedroom next door.

"That's not going to happen, certainly not now. He's in bed," I say. "Asleep."

Again the forced smile. I have the advantage of being inside the doorway and I place my leg behind the door to prevent it being fully opened. But this is still one creepy fuck and I think back to what Barry was saying earlier.

"What have you done to her?" he asks.

"What do you mean?"

"Caitlin," he says. "What did you do?" The thought crosses my mind that Imran could have had something to do with Caitlin's disappearance, perhaps to gain access to Tomas.

I don't know why this hasn't occurred to me before and if I phone PC Byrne in the morning then I shall say so.

"How did you find out where we lived?" I ask. "Did Social Services tell you?"

"Social Services?" He laughs and looks around to his friends, or are they his brothers? "I don't need Social Services to tell me where my wife and son live."

"She's not your wife," I say.

"Whatever," he shrugs. "She's not yours either."

I still believe he must have been tipped off. The thought of him knowing where we live and possibly watching Caitlin and Tomas all this time, only deciding to make a move now he knew Caitlin was out the picture? I can't believe the barring order doesn't extend to Tomas, or is that more a question of access? Caitlin would know. Either way, surely he'd have to apply through the courts?

"You're not going to see Tomas," I say flatly.

"Well, if it doesn't happen now, you know it's going to happen sooner or later. There's nothing you can do to stop me."

If anyone had asked me before tonight what I would do if Imran turned up at the flat I would have said I'd just close the door in his face. And I think with everything that's happened, I knew this moment was coming; I just wasn't expecting it tonight. Yes, I'm scared. I'm intimidated too; I think I would have been if it was simply a matter of meeting Caitlin's ex-husband. But all day long I've been faced with people – that dreadful fucking woman from Social Services, the filth – who there's no talking to. Though they seem intent on taking my son and maybe my home, they have the full backing of the law. They are the law. And in their eyes, this thug in front of me has more of a legal right to Tomas than I do. There's very little difference between them that I can see. I know I have no legal standing, I know I'm legally fucked and that without Caitlin then it's simply down to me to protect what's mine. I've nothing to lose – they're going to do what they want anyway.

I consider letting Imran in. For a long time I look at him as he shuffles from foot to foot, secure in the knowledge that he's bound to see Tomas some time in the near future.

"Wait here," I say and push the door to, not closing it completely.

I didn't go looking for this, I think, as I walk back through to the kitchen. It's not as though I've gone out of my way to allow this to happen. If anything then the opposite is true. I would have done anything to avoid this trouble coming to my door. But now it's here and I have to decide what to do.

I look at the knife I left on the side from peeling Tomas' apple. As I pick it up I'm perfectly aware of what I'm doing, almost as though I've had an earlier rehearsal and that this is when I finally get to act things out. I weigh the knife in my hand and it's not really what I need. I look along the knife rack on the wall. Our sharpest knife is not the strongest blade; I choose a knife we rarely use but it's thick and strong with a solid tip that I know won't snap or bend. I transfer the paring knife to my left hand and take the larger knife from the rack.

When I return to the front door I see that Imran has stepped inside the hallway and this arrogance makes it easier. He catches sight of the smaller knife in my left hand and laughs, happy to be on familiar ground, but he doesn't see the larger knife until it's to late. In a single upward motion I jam the knife into his side; his leather coat gives him some protection but I push in hard enough to penetrate through to his body. I can feel the knife push up from below and in hard against his body. As he reacts I bring the smaller knife up to his other side, in the small of his back to prevent him simply jumping out the way. There's no way the paring knife can cut through the leather but that's OK. I've never pushed a knife into another person before so I can't tell you much more. I know I have to be firm enough to let him know I'm serious. Once he realises the situation he's in then Imran slightly raises his arms

"Whoa," he says laughing. I get the feeling this isn't the first time he's had this happen. I push in harder.

"Get the fuck out of my house," I say. I allow him to step back, through the doorway and down to the path, still pressing hard enough to force him away from me. I follow him outside, the two knives still in place as I negotiate the doorstep. I'm aware of movement all around me and I see Imran's brothers coming through the gate. To my right, Barry appears from next door with something heavy in his hand (a hammer, I find out later) and for a second we all stay as we are.

"Push him away," Barry tells me and I do. "Leave," he then says to Imran. "You're not wanted here."

As Imran steps back to his brothers I see him consider. There are three of them after all. He holds his side and checks the tear though his jacket. I can't believe what I've just done and already the shakes and the fear are starting to hit me.

Out on the street I see John from upstairs approach along the footpath, carrying his tool kit home from work. As he sees Imran and his brothers he automatically drops his bag to the floor.

"What the fuck!" he says.

"It's alright," says Barry. "They're just leaving."

Imran nods; it's either this or take on John and Barry.

"This isn't over," he says to me.

They walk out through the gate, John holding it open as they go past and sticking his face close into Imran's. They walk across the road to their car and make a big deal out of revving the engine as they drive away.

"What the fuck were those Pakis doing here?" asks John, picking up his tool kit from the street. He asks Barry but I know the question is directed at me.

"This isn't good, Gregory," Barry says. "What the hell were you thinking? You're lucky they didn't have guns." That hadn't occurred to me and I realise I'm hopelessly out of my depth. "Do you know who that was?" he asks John.

"I don't give a shit," he says. "I just don't want any Pakis in my street." He sees the knives in my hands and laughs once. "Fucking college boy," he says and goes to his own front door. This is when I notice the hammer in Barry's hand.

"Sort it out," Barry says into my face, echoing Suzie from earlier.

Friends like these. I don't even thank them.

I close and lock the door, bolting the chain across. Sure, if somebody was determined enough then they could break through but I think it unlikely they'd go that far. I return the knives to the kitchen, checking first for blood on the larger knife. I've no idea if I actually cut into Imran; I hope I hurt him but I don't think cunts like that stay hurt for long.

I come back through to the living room. I know it's impossible for Tomas not to have heard, sleeping as he is in my bed, but I can't go and face him just yet. I sit in the armchair and think – what? How it's come to this so quickly? I know of no one I can phone or call upon to get me through this, least of all with Tomas within earshot. I'm so hopelessly ill-equipped to handle what's happened here. Ever since Monday evening when Caitlin didn't come home, through to whatever mad situation is developing now, at each turn I seem to get it wrong, or at least so not-quite-right that it makes no difference.

I reach over to the stereo and pull Springsteen's *The River* out of the stack of tapes. I rewind to 'Point Blank'. As the music plays then I hear Tomas stir. He walks calmly through from the bedroom, safe in the knowledge that there's no way he can get into trouble for getting up out of bed tonight. He climbs straight up on to my knee and into my arms and we sit together in the chair, listening to the music.

"That was my real father, wasn't it?" he asks after a while.

"Yes, it was."

"What did he want?"

"To take you away from me."

"But you wouldn't let him?"

"No," I say and then, "I don't think it's right until we know what's happened to your Mum."

"And what then?" he asks.

"Even then I don't think it would be right but it may not be my choice. We just have to hope your Mum's OK."

"Do you think she is?"

"I don't know, son. I don't know."

We sit and listen to the music. I can't think what's best to say to Tomas. "I just don't know what to do," I say.

He turns in my arms and looks at me.

"Whatever you do," he says, "it'll be OK with me."

"Thank you, my love."

"I want to stay with you, no matter what," he says.

"I know you do, Tomas, I know you do." Again, the music. And the tears flow down my face.

"Don't cry," he says.

"OK." As if I have a choice. We sit together like this for a while, tiredness taking over my body. 'Stolen Car' comes on the stereo.

"Why don't you phone your Mum?"

"Grannie Annie?" I say. This is the second time he's suggested I call my mother.

"Grandma Annie," he corrects, "don't call her that. Ask her what you should do."

"It's too late for Grandma Annie tonight," I say. "She could well be in bed asleep but maybe we'll call her in the morning?"

"Together?" asks Tomas.

"Together," I agree. "Now, come on. You get into bed and I'll be in before the music's finished." He goes off satisfied and I walk through to wash my face with cold water in the bathroom. He's right of course and only a few years ago Annie would have been the first person to call for advice but ever since Dad was killed I've not felt as free to do so. I brush my teeth, take out and clean my lenses and go through to the bedroom, switching off first Bruce, and then the lights, as I pass.

Eight

I don't know if I'm sleeping when I think I hear movement outside. I check the digital clock and see it's almost four in the morning. I lie there frozen in the near darkness; the only light is from the hallway. It didn't sound like someone trying to break in quietly. (What am I talking about? I haven't got a clue what I heard.) Beside me Tomas sleeps on. He still trusts me enough to sleep. The fact he could hold my arm with his hand was sufficient to send him off and I can hear from his breathing just how deep a sleep he's in. Despite the day he had yesterday, he seems to take our agreement at face value – that so long as we continue to cope with this together then we shall somehow be OK. Did he hear my crazy stunt with the knives; how close I came to endangering our staying together? And a mention of guns; how scared can a little boy be? But because I'm here, because he can go to sleep holding my arm, then he trusts me to keep him safe. I'm not sure I deserve this.

What have I started? Why didn't I just close the door on Imran? Surely now I've made things worse? Too hung up on asserting some imaginary line I wouldn't allow to be crossed, some notion of this being my home? It's just a council flat, for Christ's sake. What's any of it worth if I'm going to lose Tomas? If Imran and his brothers were to come back now I wouldn't stand a chance.

I strain to hear movement, anything that would let me know what's happening. Tomas sleeps on, undisturbed and oblivious. When there's no further sound, I know I have to go through to check it out, if only for peace of mind. I'm nervous about leaving Tomas but it's the only way to put my mind at rest. He stirs but doesn't wake up as I lift his hand off my arm. I walk through to the kitchen, turning on lights as I go – nothing. I double-back into Tomas's bedroom – still nothing. I turn off all the lights, including the one in the hallway, and listen in the darkness. I unlock the front door and take off the chain – is this what they want? – and I look outside. Across the road, a car revs away. I get the message. They can do what they want.

I close and lock the door, replace the chain.

Towards dawn, though there is no dawn as such, just an increasing greyness replacing the dark, I can smell smoke and jump up quickly from my bed. Tomas wakes up behind me.

"What?" he shouts.

"Stay there," I say and run through the flat but there's nothing. I stand still in the living room and, just as I'd strained to listen for noises in the night, I try to catch the smell of smoke in the air. It's in my head but I can't figure out where it's coming from. I walk back through into Tomas' bedroom, the kitchen – nothing.

"Gregory," shouts Tomas.

"One minute, son," I call back. I unlock the back door. There's nothing to see outside but a heavy, cold drizzle. Yesterday's suggestion of snow has been replaced by rain; typical Manchester.

"What is it?" asks Tomas. He's followed me through to the kitchen, his bare feet on the cold stone floor.

"Nothing, son," I say, closing and locking the back door. "I thought I could smell smoke."

He looks up without focussing and sniffs the air.

"I can't smell anything," he says.

"No," I agree and gather his shoulders in my hands as I pass by. "Let's get back into bed before we catch cold," I say.

"What time is it?" he asks as we return to the bedroom and then he checks the digital alarm clock for himself. "Six twenty-five." He covers his head with the duvet, intent on going back to sleep.

Before I get back into bed, I check one more thing. I take off the chain and unlock the front door but again I see no sign of fire. I look along to Suzie's front door, memories of the fire at number five not spreading through the walls. I look above to John and Sarah's but by now I'm beginning to believe I've imagined it. Previous dawn fires playing tricks on my memory. I can't get the smell out my head, though; it feels like it's behind my eyes.

I lock up once more and get into bed next to Tomas. I don't think he's sleeping but he seems determined to try. At least it's warm in here. I lie on my back and feel the heat calm me down. Above me, on top of the wardrobe, are the two suitcases. I don't understand whatever secret they hold; I don't know what it is they're telling me. I know Caitlin's is empty. I know the contents of my own so well I barely need to keep them as a reminder. I think today will be the day I throw all that stuff away, my diary too. What have I learnt, after all – that I had a good thing with Brenda and I blew it? That she loved me and I betrayed her trust by acting like a prick? I'd have done the same to Caitlin last night – made the same mistake – if only Olivia hadn't had to leave. And Leta – did I learn anything there, really?

Another dawn, later than dawn really but early on a summer morning. I can't sleep past the dawn these days; I have nothing to get up for but I can't stay in my bed. I'm showering and I hear the bell ring downstairs. I hear the familiar sounds of the door being answered by either Roger or Mary from the rooms below. I'm surprised that anyone else should be awake, let alone out making calls, but then I guess it's time for people to get ready for work. I'm even more surprised when, from what I can make out from the noises on the stairs, I realise that the visitor is looking for me. It could only be one person and I move my head from under the shower to listen. There are voices below. I hear Mary's reluctance, some complaint about the hour that I know is about more than time. The water hits the back of my neck and runs down my body as I hear Leta climb the extra steps to my floor. She taps on the bathroom door.

"Gregory, it's me."

I call out over the noise of the shower.

"Do you want to go through to the bedroom? I'll be out in a moment."

Part of me is excited – isn't this what I would have asked for? But I take my time beneath the shower, let the water flow and hopefully help me think this through. I realise I'm stronger, mentally, than I have been in a long while and this gives me the confidence to turn off the shower and get dry. I know it's decision time but I still don't know what my decision will be. I don't have any clothes in the bathroom so I wrap the towel around my waist and walk through to my room.

"Hi," I say.

"Hi Gregory," Leta replies, and we both smile at my not being dressed.

"You can look away if it's too much temptation," I say. I pull on my jeans and t-shirt.

"I don't think Mary was too pleased to see me," she says.

"No," I agree.

"Looking after her Gregory?"

"She's concerned is all."

"I know, I was just kidding." Weirdly – now I have the business of getting dressed out the way – it seems more awkward for us both to be standing in my room.

"Would you like a cup of tea or coffee?" I ask.

"No, I…" she begins. "No thank you."

I nod at the chair, inviting Leta to sit down, but she stays standing. I sit on the bed.

"How have you been?" she says.

"OK," I shrug. "Getting by. Missing you but getting by."

"I've been desperate," she says laughing – but it's not a real laugh.

Yeah well, I think, you had that coming.

"Not like my name at all." Leta means happiness, or so she once told me. "But I guess it's nothing more than I deserve."

I'm not arguing.

"I wanted to come and see you," she says. "Strange time of day, I know, but I found myself outside so I knocked and then Mary let me in."

I look up at her and see that she looks like shit; as beautiful as ever but still like shit.

"When you didn't reply to my letter, I presumed that meant you didn't want to see me."

"I'm glad you came," I say.

"Are you? Really?"

"Of course. How could I not be?"

"I thought you might never want to see me again?"

"I'm in love with you. How could I not want to see you again?"

"Still?" she asks. "After all I've done?"

"I might not be able to see you again," I say, "but I'm never going to stop wanting to see you."

Leta nods in understanding. We're both quiet for a while.

"How's the writing going?" she asks, looking at the typewriter set up on the table.

"It's not really," I admit. "Nothing worth talking about anyway."

"What are you going to do, Gregory? You can't carry on like this forever."

This is an old argument and we both know it.

"I'll carry on for as long as I can then," I say. Why is my earning money, or not earning money, such a big deal to Leta? She earns enough to support herself and I've never asked her to help support me. "It would have been enough for me just to be your lover," I say.

"But you can't build a future on that."

"It's not a bad place to start."

"But what if we were to have children – what would happen then? How would we live?"

"Is that what you wanted – for us to have children?" I ask.

"Eventually, yes, of course."

"Then I would have done whatever I had to do at the time."

"You mean get a job? Work for a living?"

"If that was what was required," I say, "yes."

"But that would have been the death of you," says Leta.

"Not if I could be with you."

She doesn't say anything; I don't either. As I say, an old argument.

"What do you want?" I ask when it's apparent that neither of us is about to speak. "Why have you come here?"

"To say I'm sorry," says Leta.

Sorry for what – for seeing Sutcliffe again? Sorry for deciding that I wasn't enough for her? Sorry I wasn't the one to help her break her addiction to Sutcliffe?

"You don't have to do that," I say.

Sorry for her lies and stories – none of which I shall ever know were true? Sorry for making me fall in love with her, for the hurt and for the deceit? Sorry for the future? For my future and how I'll never be free of this past?

I stand up and put my arms around her. She's crying; she's sorry. I hold her but it's not going to change a thing. We kiss and undress. We have sex, make love; it'd be crazy not to. As I come inside her she looks at me silently. She knows she has everything I have to give. We both know it's for the last time.

Caitlin listens to Imran breathing next to her in the bed. She holds her own breath when he wakes up and she listens to the ordinariness of his movements. She pretends to be asleep as he washes and dresses for work. She can't stand another scene, can't go through with the begging for forgiveness and the tears of shame and regret. She hasn't slept or moved all night. She's in too much pain to move and knows well enough to wait for Imran to leave before checking her injuries. Eventually he goes without saying a word. This in itself is a first; perhaps he knows that there's no undoing what happened last night. Or maybe this is how Imran sees their future life together – a future of threats and violence – because he knows she doesn't have the strength to fight?

Caitlin lifts her head from the pillow and swings her legs across the bed to the floor. Her head is pounding and it's this that she sees to first. She walks slowly and painfully from the bedroom. She finds painkillers in the bathroom cabinet and swallows them with the help of some water, scooping the water in her hand from the tap. Her lips are swollen and the water drips down her chin, like drool at the dentist. She looks in the mirror and can see that the whole of one side of her face is distorted. She wets a cloth with cold water and dabs at her face; she thinks it could have been a lot worse.

The blood from the cut between her legs has stained her nightshirt and the bedclothes. She can feel where it has dried on her overnight and is reluctant to clean it for fear of opening up the cut once more. She does though, again dabbing with the wet cloth and using a sanitary towel to stem the flow. She thinks about checking the cut by holding her make-up mirror down below her knees but then she decides not to dwell on her injuries; she's afraid that might break down her resolve and her determination to leave.

The thought of just presenting herself at the hospital crosses her mind again – this time with even greater justification – but it's having to think of answers to the questions she knows they will ask that puts her off. Over-riding everything is the need to leave this city, to get away from Imran and to make sure that her baby is safe. Perhaps when she arrives in Manchester a hospital will be as good a place as any to start, but after that she's going to need a safe place to hide. If she can just see her baby born safely then maybe she'll be strong enough to face whatever comes next. More and more the idea of asking for help at a hospital becomes fixed in her mind; if they can't help then maybe they know who can?

Nothing is easy but at least the clarity of her situation gives Caitlin the strength to pack her bag again and to set off on the journey to the station. She chooses fewer clothes for her suitcase but it's still a pull on her arms and back. She can hardly leave with nothing though; once she leaves the house then she's no idea where any future money may come from.

She locks the door and posts the keys back through the letterbox. It seems a casual way to say goodbye to the house she shared with Imran. It's not without regret, but she realises that for her own sake and for the sake of her baby, this can never be her home now. Fighting for what might be rightfully hers is not an option; it's too high a price to pay.

No taxi into town today. She knows she looks a fright, and

the other passengers on the bus look away, but this is not the issue now: getting away is everything. So, no dark glasses, no attempt to hide her injuries. She has a little money, salvaged from various places in the house – small amounts of cash left laying around by Imran – enough to see her through today and then tomorrow can look after tomorrow. At least the bus drops her fairly close to the station and her walk there is easier than the arduous trek up Woodhouse Lane last night. It's very different here this morning; there are fewer people and less of a rush and it's not quite as intimidating in the daylight.

She fingers her unused train ticket. The uncertainty remains – she has nowhere to go once she gets to Manchester and she knows that Imran can find her there every bit as easily as here. But having failed yesterday, there's no question of not boarding the train today. So she stands on the platform and waits, suitcase by her feet.

I soon realise that Tomas is feigning using sleep to avoid going to school. His idea of what he must look like while he's sleeping makes me smile.

"Tomas," I say. "I'm going to make myself a cup of tea but then it will be time to move." He doesn't reply. I lift the bedclothes from over his face; his eyes are closed but there's movement there behind the lids. "We have those phone calls to make, remember?" He pulls the duvet back up and turns over, away from me. When I return with my tea, he's still in the same position. I sit with him for a while, waiting for him to come round.

"I don't want to go to school," he says eventually, his voice muffled by the bedding. I rest my hand on his shoulder.

"We have no choice, son," I say. "You saw what happened yesterday. If I don't take you to school then I'm going to be in even deeper trouble than I am already."

"Are you in trouble?" he asks, looking at me for the first time.

"I mean things will be worse than they already are," I say.

"How could they be?" he asks. He's got the blues and who

can blame him? After what he's been through, I can't begrudge him this.

"Come on Tomas, today's Friday – just one more day and then we have the weekend together."

"I don't want to go," he repeats. "What if you're not there to pick me up?" Memories of the other day – he's not going to forget so quickly.

"I'll be there," I promise but my credit rating isn't too high. "I spoke to the policeman yesterday; I don't think they'll ask me to do the same today."

"What if they do?"

"Then I'll tell them I have to be at school for you. They can't argue with that. What's more likely is that I'll be in trouble if I don't take you to school."

"In trouble with the police?"

"Just – in trouble," I say.

I leave him be while I have a wash and then bring him in a damp face-cloth; as a concession, he can get by with a cat-lick this morning. I carry his clothes through from his own room.

"Your clothes are there," I tell him but he doesn't respond from beneath the duvet. "Tomas," I say again and then "Tomas!" I feel bad for shouting at him but I can't be late for school, not today. He moves and I leave him be to get dressed alone.

I pick up the phone and dial the number for Grannie Annie, my mother. There's no danger of her not being awake; ever since Dad died she's been an early bird, sometimes up as early as five in the morning. Then in the evening, soon after seven, she's asleep in her chair before dragging herself off to bed. I can't imagine what it must be like for her but then that's partly because I'm never there. My brothers and sisters all live closer to home; only I moved away to college. I get the impression they call in regularly; one sister calls in at least once a day. They all know I couldn't possibly do that but they also know I could do a lot more. The distance is my justification but the only justifying I do is to myself; the others, including Grannie Annie, don't seem to mind and never make anything of it.

I created the distance. I created the distance because I had to get away from home – from my father really – and then when he died it became harder and harder ever to go back. Of course I did, first for the funeral, and then more often with Tomas and Caitlin, but the distance seemed to grow and grow. Tomas in particular makes it easier to be there but he also gives me an excuse to stay away – I have my own family now. It's as though I can visit under cover, in disguise. The two occasions that Annie has tried talking to me – the first time she'd told me I had no reason to feel bad about my father dying, it was sad but nobody's fault; the second she said how proud he would have been of how I was with Tomas – I've used Tomas's presence as an excuse not to talk.

"Nobody's fault," I remember saying to Caitlin on the train journey home that time. "How about the dumb-fuck motorcyclist that killed him?"

"Stop beating yourself up over it," she said and looked out the window at the snow on the hills. I don't think we ever talked about it again.

I place the receiver down after only a couple of rings, before Annie has chance to pick up the phone.

"Are you phoning Grandma?" asks Tomas as he comes through to the living room. He's dressed.

"There was no reply," I lie. "We'll try later."

"Try again now," he says.

"No, later. She's only going to tell me to do exactly as the police say. Can you remember Rosie and Bill's number – I'm about to phone that policewoman." It's a male voice that answers so I ask for PC Byrne.

"She's not in until eight-thirty. Can I help?"

I give my name.

"Can I leave a phone number for her?" I ask.

"Oh, hang on," he says. "You can speak to her yourself." He hands over the phone.

"PC Byrne."

I give her the number, as called out by Tomas. If Grannie Annie's advice would be to cooperate with the police, then maybe this is what I should do.

"We were thinking," I say looking at Tomas, "that another possibility may be Caitlin's parents. She hasn't seen them for a long while but there's an outside chance – "

"We checked," she interrupts, "and nothing."

"You already contacted them?" I ask. "What was their reaction?" What must have been their reaction, the police calling for Caitlin after all these years?

"They had no idea where she may be," says PC Byrne. Tomas is looking up at me so I shake my head and he looks away in disappointment. "I'm not sure they cared too much either," she adds.

"No? Sorry – one second." I cover the mouthpiece with my hand and speak to Tomas. "Your breakfast is set out in the kitchen. I don't want to be late for school." He goes through reluctantly; I think he's had enough of being good for a while. "PC Byrne," I say quietly. I'm not sure this is what I should be calling her.

"Mr Isaacs?"

"Tomas's father came here last night, looking to cause trouble."

"Oh dear," she says, "that's not right."

"Oh dear?" I start but then I stop myself. "I – " I don't know how to put it without sounding like a conspiracy theorist. "Can you see why I find it hard to cooperate when things like that happen?" I ask.

"We can speak to him again," she says. "Make it clear he's not to – "

"Speak to him again?"

"Well, naturally we had to ask him if he knew where Ms O'Connor might be."

"But that was all the encouragement he needed," I say. "Now he knows Caitlin's missing, he's sniffing 'round Tomas already."

"There's no way he can gain access to your son," she says. "Not without going through the courts."

"That's not the impression that woman from Social Services gave me yesterday. And it's not going to make much of a difference to the likes of Tomas's father." I try to lower my voice for this last bit.

"As I said, we'll have another word. He won't bother you again."

"If anything happens to Tomas – "

"Please, Mr Isaacs, calm down. Please just try to keep calm. If you manage to – "

"I think she's killed herself," I say.

"We don't know – "

"We don't know anything do we?" Christ, this isn't what I called to say.

"Mr Isaacs, is Tomas there with you?"

"He's in the kitchen," I say.

"Good, because he doesn't need to hear this. You know that the best thing you can do for him is to keep your head and be as reassuringly normal as possible. Now I appreciate you calling and I understand that none of this is easy for you but if you can continue on in your daily routine then that will allow us to look for Ms O'Connor." I hear her but I don't reply. The silence from the kitchen tells me Tomas is listening hard to what I have to say. "Mr Isaacs?"

"Yes," I say. "We're up and on our way to school right now."

"Good," she says. "Call me on this number if you need me through the day."

Tomas has finished his cereal when I look in on him in the kitchen. I don't know how much he heard.

"Can we try Grandma Annie again?" he asks.

"No," I say.

"Please."

"No," I say again. "We'll try this afternoon. Come on, brush your teeth and we'll go." He looks so unhappy but still he does as he's told. What's more, it's one of those miserably wet days outside, cold and windy; if ever there was a day to stay off school then it's today. As I shut the gate behind us though, I've reason to be thankful for the weather. Tomas is sheltering his face from the wind and the rain, holding down the hood of his coat. He doesn't see the graffiti scrawled along the front of the building:

"Paki Mafia Rule."

We're on time for school but only because a bus arrives as we're passing the stop. I don't feel like walking at Tomas' pace in this bad weather so we jump on the bus and we arrive at school even earlier than usual. They're letting the kids in early to shelter from the weather and the playground area is empty but for a few children running across to the entrance of the school. Behind me at the school gates, a few parents watch from their cars; others beside me wait for their kids to get inside, willing them to hurry on so we can all get out the rain. Everybody waits until their children are safely inside the school. I can see the head teacher standing in the school doorway, sharing a joke with a parent.

Very chummy, I think to myself, remembering our little exchange from yesterday.

But then, to my horror, I realise it's Imran she's talking to. I can't believe it – surely this isn't right? I don't know what's happening here but it figures – knowing what I know about Imran – that he'd endear himself to that old bitch. I call Tomas back from across the yard but he doesn't hear me.

"Tomas!" I shout louder and he stops to turn around.

I walk over to him; conscious that Imran and the head teacher are watching me from the doorway. Tomas is expecting to be handed something he's forgotten.

"I've changed my mind," I say. "I think you should stay off school today."

He turns to face the head teacher; the hood of his coat means he has to fully turn his body to look in the other direction. I grab his hand and pull against him towards the school gates. He resists my pull – now he's here, he feels he might as well go in. I keep walking back towards the gates and Tomas tags reluctantly along behind.

"Why?" he asks.

"I'll tell you in a moment," I say.

I know my behaviour is erratic but I have to get away from the school. I know I'm creating a bit of a scene – the parents at the gate are curious – but I think I have the weather on my side; I don't think the head teacher will follow me out into the rain. If I had a car then this is the moment I would get in it and drive, get as far away as possible and put as great a distance as I could between the school and myself. But I don't have a car; I can't even drive and the only thing I can think of is to jump on another bus.

"Come on," I say to Tomas. He hesitates but then follows me as I run for a bus pulling up to a stop along the road.

"This is going the wrong way," he says as we wait to pay.

"I know. You get on and find a seat and I'll explain in a moment." The bus is full with passengers travelling into town for work and we share a seat, Tomas standing in the space between my legs.

"I changed my mind," I repeat. I can't tell him why. "You were right," I say. "We should go to Grannie Annie's – Grandma Annie's," I correct myself. I suggest his grandma as a way of placating Tomas but maybe there's something in this, a way to get back at least a little control?

"Right now? What about school? Will you get into trouble?"

"I'll phone the school and explain," I say. I need to present this to Tomas as being in some way acceptable or normal behaviour.

"What about the police?" he asks.

"I'll call them too," I say. I know I've over-stepped the mark but there's no way I'm about hand Tomas over with Imran at the school. Like pulling off the knife stunt last night, I don't know what I've done here but it's done now so – what? Maybe going to my mother's isn't such a bad idea; give myself time and space to think this all through? It doesn't look good though, I know it doesn't look good and I've changed something here – how will what I've done be seen?

It's uncomfortable on the bus in our wet clothes. Tomas is full of questions – how will his grandma know we're going? Have we enough money to get there? What about a change of clothes? And most pertinent of all – what if his mum comes home and we're not there? I cover for the inadequacy of my plan as best I can but the truth is I'm losing it, clueless out here in the world. Perhaps my own mother will help put me right? As we approach town I decide to jump off at the top of Oxford Road and cut through along the canal to the station. I've no wish to pass by the police station and besides, this is the more direct route.

As we arrive at the station I check my pocket for change, deciding it's best to call home before I buy the tickets. But then I realise I'm dependent on being able to use my credit card to pay – a credit card with no credit that will only work if they don't check for authorisation. They were foolish enough to offer me a credit card in the first place – let them worry about it. I pay for the tickets and then I call home.

My mother's pleased but surprised; I can hear the unspoken questions in her voice. I tell her I'll explain when we arrive.

"What did she say?" asks Tomas.

"It's fine," I say, " she'll see us there." He doesn't need to know any more. My mind is racing. I dial Roger and Mary's number.

"Mary," I say to the answer machine. She will be sleeping and Roger will have left for work. "Tomas and I are going to my mother's for a few days. Caitlin's still not back." I pause for a second. "Could yourself and Roger call over to the flat at some point, just in case Caitlin returns while we're away?" I'm not sure the answer machine works; it's new but untrustworthy. The message is as much for Tomas as for Roger and Mary; Caitlin won't be coming home. "We'll call Mary again from Grandma's," I add to Tomas as I replace the receiver.

Now for the hard part – there's no way I'm phoning the school – fuck them! I find the card that PC Byrne gave to me yesterday and I dial her number. It takes a while to get put through and I'm conscious of my money running low. Tomas is sat on a bench a few feet away, within listening distance.

"Mr Isaacs?"

"I've – I didn't take Tomas to school," I say, "and I wanted to let you know."

"Why?" Her voice is flat, expressionless.

"Tomas's father was there, with his teacher. I don't think that's right."

"When was this?" she asks.

"Just now, this morning, at around nine when I dropped Tomas for school."

"I don't think so; I was speaking to him at home at around that time."

I don't understand her; I saw him. It had to be him.

"What did you do?" she asks.

I describe our flight into town.

"So where are you now?" she asks.

I tell her.

"One minute," she says and I hear her talking with the mouthpiece covered. I put some more money in for the phone.

"Mr Isaacs." It's the detective, Sand. "I'm not sure what you're thinking of doing but I want you to stop and consider for a while."

"I'm taking Tomas to my mother's," I say.

"And I can understand why," he agrees "but I would ask you again to stop and consider. This isn't going to help. Taking Tomas and – "

"I'm not taking Tomas," I say. "I mean, I am taking him but not like that."

"I was going to say, taking him from school – it's not going to go down too well."

"I can't help that now," I say.

"No but let us help you present it in a better light. Where are you now – in Piccadilly Station you say?" I hear PC Byrne in the background. "Come along to the office here," he suggests. "Bring Tomas; we have to find a way to sort out this mess. Please Mr Isaacs, for Tomas's sake, let's not make this worse than it is."

The pips sound again for more money and I put in my last bit of change. The phone isn't going to allow me the time to think this through. I can't figure out the connection between the school, the police, Social Services and Imran.

"I don't trust you," I say simply. I can hear Sand breathing down the line. I turn in towards the phone booth, away from Tomas. "I'm scared," I say. I am scared.

"Then come in here and let's talk," he says.

"I'm scared I may have done something – to Caitlin."

"Mr Isaacs – "

The pips sound again and I let the line go dead. I gather myself for a second or so and then turn around to Tomas.

"Come on, son." We go through for the train.

I can see that Tomas isn't too sure about this. He's happy to be going to his Grandma's but not without all his things, his clothes and some toys. I'm in such a rush to catch this one train, to be on my way out of Manchester, that I forget even to buy him a comic to read. He has a few schoolbooks in his bag but after looking at these for a while he's quickly bored and restless. While I may have a sense of going home, of returning to what I know, Tomas is leaving the only home he's known.

"We'll just stay a day or two," I say. "Give me chance to talk to Annie and sort things out."

Tomas smiles but it's not convincing; this is a very worried little boy. I'm at such a loss that I believe only Annie can help me now. I'm grateful to Tomas for putting the idea in my head but travelling all the way to see her is too weird for him by far. He looks out the window, back towards Manchester, and remains quiet.

As the train climbs out of Manchester, we emerge from the heavy mist that's resting on the city. You'd think the weather would be worse up here but the higher we go, the clearer it becomes before we disappear into the darkness of a tunnel. Tomas puts his fingers in his ears to block out the noise but doesn't laugh along in the way he normally does. Unlike the weather, his mood is sinking deeper into the gloom. Even the snow on the hills as we emerge from the tunnel does nothing to lift his spirits.

I can't stop measuring my actions by the effect they would have in some theoretical custody hearing. Is this a responsible thing to do, to travel to Annie's for help? I think so but it probably doesn't look that way, not after taking Tomas away from school and then running from the police. I doubt if I'd get within a whiff of a custody hearing; I have no rights. All I seem to have in my favour now is possession of Tomas.

Caitlin is travelling on a different train in the opposite direction, towards Manchester. The motion of the train is reassuring, as is the noise of the wheels on the track. She knows she can't run from Imran forever, particularly if Manchester is the only place she can run. Each time the train enters one of the many dark tunnels though, and the noise increases to become the only thought in her head, she feels herself become increasingly lost, increasingly invisible to the world. She's creating distance, from Imran and their life together in Leeds, and with that distance comes the time she needs to think what she has to do next.

She's uncomfortable on the seat. There's not really enough space between the seat and the table so she tries to sit sideways on, with her back to the window, but this adds to the pain in her side. There are very few passengers travelling on this mid-week, mid-morning train – a very different experience to how it would have been the previous evening. There's a couple on the seat opposite and a few other passengers scattered throughout the carriage. As they emerge from a tunnel Caitlin is surprised by the snow on the hills, by how her view is transformed. She realises it's not simply the forty miles of the journey or the hour's duration travelling; the physical bulk of these white hills increases her sense of dislocation. Do they qualify as mountains or are they just a range of hills? Whatever, they create a barrier that the train cuts through and travels over, sometimes around, and they're still there once the train has moved on. Caitlin faces away from the direction of the train and watches the huge hills recede into the distance.

The guard enters the carriage and calls to see tickets. Caitlin takes out her purse and retrieves the single ticket she bought for her aborted journey yesterday. As he reaches her seat, she holds out the ticket. He punches a hole in it, but then hesitates and checks it once again.

"When did you buy this ticket?" he asks.

Caitlin's hand is still held up to receive the ticket; she lets it drop to her side.

"Yesterday," she says. "Yesterday evening."

"Then you can't travel on it today," says the guard.

"But the man at the – the man checked it as I came on the platform."

"Then he should have seen it was yesterday's ticket. A single ticket must be used on the day of purchase."

"But I couldn't use it," says Caitlin. A panic starts to overcome her. She's aware of being the focus of attention for the few other passengers on the train; she can't look at them and she can't bring herself to look at the guard. She's conscious again of her physical state, not just of her size but also of her face, of what must be so obvious to the whole carriage. She looks out the window and the whiteness of the snow adds to the blindness she feels behind her eyes; black spots blur her vision.

"Miss?" says the guard. "Miss? I have to ask you to buy another ticket."

"But I – " A thickness in her throat prevents Caitlin from speaking. She knew this would happen, that she'd get so far and no further. This was why she'd preferred to walk home yesterday rather than ask directions for the bus station in Leeds – anything was better than having to ask for help. To have come so far and now this; would he throw her off at the next station or force her to go back to Leeds?

"I've no money," she says. "I didn't know." She's crying but she doesn't want this to be the point.

"Nevertheless," he says. "Your ticket isn't valid."

"But I have to get to Manchester."

"Not with this ticket, I'm afraid." He turns to the couple on the seats opposite Caitlin, reaching for their tickets and clipping them almost without looking. "I'll come back to you," he says to Caitlin.

"Is there a problem?" asks the woman as she's handed back her tickets. She has a loud voice and it seems to include the whole carriage in the issue. The guard shakes his head, no, and continues on down the carriage. The woman looks over at Caitlin and then calls out after him.

"Excuse me, young man. This lady is obviously in some distress." He stops and returns to their seats. "What's the problem?" the woman says, first to the guard and then to Caitlin.

"Please don't," whispers Caitlin.

"She hasn't got a valid ticket," says the guard. His manner says what's it to you?

"But she's clearly upset," the woman says.

Caitlin wants to die; not to die of embarrassment, but to die. A sob escapes and as she tries to catch her breath, it sounds out as a rasping, grating intake of air. She covers her face in her hands and rocks in her seat. She shuts her eyes tight against the world; whatever's going on out there she wants no part of it. She tries to think again of the baby inside her, to find the strength she's found there before, but it seems a long time ago and hard to find. Was it really so much to ask, to have a family of her own? She'd never reckoned on there being such a high price to pay.

"She has a single ticket but it was purchased yesterday," says the guard.

"Oh for God's sake, man," says the woman. She stands up, brushing past the guard and takes the seat facing Caitlin. She's a large woman and yet moves with confidence and agility on the moving train. "If she has a ticket then she has a ticket," she says to the guard. "If you're so intent on making her pay again then we shall pay for her – Bill?" She calls over to her partner, who nods in agreement. "But I'm not sure you're right," she adds to the guard. "Where are you travelling to my dear?" she asks Caitlin.

"She has a ticket for Manchester," says the guard.

"And so do we," says the woman. "When we arrive – if you still wish to make her pay again – then we shall check to see if it's absolutely necessary." She turns again to Caitlin, more or less dismissing the guard through sheer strength of will.

He places Caitlin's ticket on the table and walks away to the next passenger in the carriage.

"There now," says the woman to Caitlin, "there now." She reaches over and rubs her hand along Caitlin's upper arm. Caitlin lets her hands fall from her face but her eyes remain shut.

"Thank you," she says quietly.

"Not at all," the woman says. "Not at all. You just have a rest now before we get to Manchester. You look all in, dear."

When Caitlin opens her eyes, she sees the woman shake her head in the direction of her partner, Bill, and indicate with her hand to her face. The woman, aware that Caitlin has seen her, reaches out again and this time finds Caitlin's hand.

"When's your baby due, dear – soon?"

"In a week or so," says Caitlin. She wipes her wet face with the sleeve of her coat.

"You have to look after yourself, sweetie. Have you somewhere to go when you get to Manchester? Is there anyone there to meet you?" The unspoken hope is that Caitlin is running away from and not returning to whoever's done this to her face.

Caitlin shakes her head.

"I'm going to go to the hospital, I think," she says.

"Good for you, my dear, good for you. We can help you if you like, can't we Bill? That's my Bill over there," she says to Caitlin, "and I'm Rosie. You tell me now if you want me to mind my own business. Tell me to get lost if that's what you want."

"No," says Caitlin.

Rosie lowers her voice and speaks quietly to Caitlin.

"Bill is a gentleman," she says, " as in, a gentle man. But if you'd prefer to be left alone, then just you say."

"No," says Caitlin again.

Rosie continues to speak in a low tone.

"You need to get to somewhere safe, my dear," she says. "I don't know what's happened to you but you need to find somewhere safe."

Caitlin closes her eyes again and lets the tiredness take over.

"That's right sweetie, you have a rest," she hears Rosie say. She falls into a deep sleep, reassured again by the noise and motion of the train.

But when she wakes up she's confused because she's still on the platform in Leeds station and she's beginning to fear that she might never get away. Train after train arrives but she never leaves. She looks around for her suitcase but it's not there. She remembers Imran taking it from her hand. Is he here at the station; has he caught up with her already? She touches her hand to the swelling on her face but there's nothing to feel – just her dry lips – and she's scared now because she distinctly remembers being hit. And she remembers leaving this morning and then being on the train – but how, when she's still here?

Nine

As the train pulls into Leeds station, I can see Caitlin standing on the opposite platform. She has her back to us but she's looking along the tracks and I catch a glimpse of her face.

I should be surprised but I'm not. It makes perfect sense – where else would she go but back into her past? I understand now why Caitlin's suitcase has been so much on my mind this past week. But could she really have been here all this time – brought back by all our recent upsets to what must still be the single worst moment of her life?

Then as the train moves by I think I may have been mistaken. For years after Brenda finished with me, I imagined seeing her everywhere. I would catch sight of her and say hello; she'd agree to forgive me and promise to give me a second chance. My need to see Brenda was so strong that it really happened in my mind – only in time did I finally accept that I was never going to see her again. I'm scared that I may be doing the same thing now with Caitlin. And Imran – who did I see this morning if I didn't see Imran? Was it just another Paki? Am I losing it?

Our train stops and I look through the window but if Caitlin is out there, then she's too far back along the platform to be seen from here.

"What is it?" asks Tomas.

"Come on," I say, standing up. "We have to get off."

"Why?" he asks, not moving.

"Come on, I'll explain." I'm conscious that the train will move off at any moment.

"No," he says.

I can't tell him what I think I've seen. I'm beginning to fear it doesn't make any sense after all – it would make even less sense to Tomas – and what if I'm wrong? I can't raise his hopes only to have them beaten out of him again. But I have to check; however crazy it may seem, I have to check.

"Tomas," I say.

"No, I'm not getting off the train. We're going to Grandma Annie's."

"Tomas, I just have to check something, please. If we go now then we can jump straight back on to the train before it leaves."

"No."

It's too strange; he's followed me away from school and agreed to come with me on the train but this is one step too far. He hunches down further into his seat.

Already I feel the other passengers listening; I see a few are watching. I lean over to Tomas and speak quietly.

"Tomas, please."

"No."

I have seconds to make up my mind. I grab him under the arms and lift him from his seat. It's not as though he's a baby and his legs are caught beneath the table. I pull harder.

"No!" he screams and lifts his legs out to kick at my stomach. I pull him closer to me and hold him tight. "My bag," he shouts.

"Forget it," I say and start to carry him along the carriage to the door. If I was a woman carrying her brat of a child from the train then everyone would pretend to ignore me and breathe a sigh of relief once we were gone. But I'm not a woman and I'm not Tomas' mother; I'm not even his father. I can see that the passengers think there's something unusual about Tomas being carried from the train crying and against his will. I'm not too sure myself that this isn't somehow wrong. A few passengers stir uncertainly but no one moves to stop me. Holding Tomas still in one hand, I manage to open the carriage door. I step down and slam the door shut behind us. He's stopped resisting now but he's crying tears of resentment – at me, at everything. I put him down on the platform.

"I hate you," he shouts into my face.

The train is about to leave but there's no way I'm getting back on that particular train. I stand apart from Tomas on the platform and let him cry himself out. There's no shortage of passers-by giving us disapproving looks as they wonder just what is going on here. Tomas is so loud but there's nothing I can do; if I try to shush him then it's going to make him worse. The guard blows his whistle and the train starts to move. Once it's obvious to Tomas, once he knows for sure that he won't be on that train, then he calms a little and I pass him a tissue. I let him hate me for a while.

When I think he's ready, I kneel down on the platform to speak to him. He looks away, to the side, not interested in what I have to say. The last carriage passes us by, leaving a clear view across the station to the other platforms I have my back to the tracks and, more than anything, I want to turn to see if I'm right or wrong. If Caitlin isn't there than I've done this to Tomas for no good reason at all. I'm scared to look in case I'm mistaken and – at the same time – I have to give Tomas my full attention. Dragging him from the train like that was wrong; I don't know how to try and win him back. He looks at me once and I know from his face that I've lost him, that this time I've gone too far. But then he looks past me, over my shoulder to the opposite platform and his eyes return to my own in confusion. I know without looking what he's seen.

"Mum?" He looks again from me to his mother across the tracks.

I stand up and turn around. I can see Caitlin; she's about twenty yards away, looking along the tracks at a train that's about to arrive at her platform. She takes a few steps towards the oncoming train. I can see that she's talking, muttering quietly to herself.

"Mum!" shouts Tomas and Caitlin stops for a second to listen but then continues in some private conversation she's having with herself. Even from this distance I can see that Caitlin's lips are parched and dry; wherever she's been then she must be seriously dehydrated. I can see that exhaustion is pulling at her body but something inside her, some inner reserve of strength, is keeping her going with this determined debate.

Tomas looks up at me.

"Can she hear me?" he asks.

"Try again," I say. The train pulling into the platform behind Caitlin is making it hard for Tomas to be heard. We're both aware of the very real danger that Caitlin may be about to board the train – or worse, I think – and that there's every chance we're about to lose her again.

"Mum!" he shouts, as loud as he can.

"Caitlin!"

Again she stops to listen and this time she turns to look our way. She looks directly at us for a second or two and Tomas half raises his hand; but then she turns away and looks back down the track.

"Mum," says Tomas again. He looks up at me in puzzlement and tries again. I put a hand on his shoulder. He can't understand why she would look at us and not react; how she could look at us and yet still not see us. But as Caitlin continues her private conversation on the opposite platform then I can see that she's in no fit state to know what's happening. She's here but she's not here; she's there but she's not there.

"Come on," I say to Tomas. I grab his hand and start to run towards the bridge across the platforms This time Tomas doesn't resist and I know that we're back in this together. If we can at least get close to Caitlin then she may recognise Tomas; more than anything we want to make sure she doesn't get on that train.

"Excuse me, sir?"

Two coppers – or what look like coppers, maybe they're the station police – approach us and block our way to the steps. I guess at first that someone has reported me for dragging Tomas from the train.

"It's OK," I say. "He's with me; I'm his Dad."

Tomas glances up at them but carries on making his way to the bridge. I have to hold his hand tight to stop him from running off because there's no way I can just barge past these coppers. I'm glad that Tomas and I are over our fight; if some busybody took exception to what was happening a few minutes before then it's obviously over and done with now. Tomas is agitated but he's not being forcibly held against his will. He looks across at Caitlin and tugs impatiently at my hand but I know that the calmer I am then the quicker we'll be.

"Mr Isaacs?" says one of the coppers.

"Yes," I say but how do they know my name?

"We'd like you to come with us, please."

There are two of them and they're big. Tomas is pulling me away and I'm tempted to let him go free while I explain but if Caitlin doesn't recognise him or has boarded the train then that would leave Tomas alone on the platform.

"Tomas," I say. "Just one second, please."

"But my Mum," he says.

"I know but just wait for one second."

"Mr Isaacs, we've been asked to detain you while we wait for our colleagues from Manchester."

So it's not about the scene on the platform.

"It's OK," I say again. "We were looking for Tomas's mother and we've found her. She's over there."

Tomas is becoming frantic, looking over at Caitlin. The coppers look down at him and then at each other, not knowing what to make of it.

"Mum!" Tomas shouts.

She's still there and it doesn't look as though she's about to get on the train. I look from Caitlin to Tomas to the police and then back at Caitlin. I can see that another train is about to arrive at our platform and that this will block off our view of Caitlin.

"There," I say, pointing her out.

"I don't know anything about that," says the copper. "We were told that if you left the train we were to detain you until they arrive from Manchester."

Tomas is beginning to realise that the coppers aren't going to let us through.

"But my Mum," he says again, this time up to one of the coppers.

"I don't know what you've done," says the copper, "but I'm afraid you're going to have to come with us."

"If you wanted to get off the train," says the other copper, laughing, "you could have done it a lot quieter – the whole station heard you."

The train pulls into the platform beside us and as Tomas loses sight of Caitlin then he relaxes his grip on my hand.

"If I can just explain," I say. "Tomas's mother has been missing and the police were worried for her safety. We were on our way to York but then we saw her, so we got off the train. If you contact them in Manchester then they'll tell you."

"We were just told to hold you," says the first copper. "If you'd stayed on the train until York then you'd have been detained there."

"But there's no need now because we've found her," I say.

"Nevertheless," he says, "if you can come this way please?"

"But could we just go across the bridge to see her? I think she needs help."

"When they arrive from Manchester, yes. Now please, we have an office here on the station and I'd much prefer not to make a huge scene."

And that's the thing isn't it? Because I have Tomas with me then I don't make a scene. He needs me to be calm and reassuring and as we walk passively along with the police then I try to explain.

"These police don't know what's been happening so we have to wait for the others to arrive from Manchester. Then we'll go and find your Mum."

"But what if she got on the train?" he asks.

"If she did then they'll be able to meet her in Manchester," I say. "They still think something might have happened to her but we'll tell them when they arrive."

The coppers walk along by our side. It seems casual and friendly enough but I know this will change if I to try making a break for it. They lead us over to a fairly nondescript office at the side of the main concourse. I can see that it's nothing more than a holding room, barely large enough for the two coppers and us to stand up in. At the doorway, Tomas slips his hand from mine and runs back towards the platform.

"Tomas!"

I turn to reach for him but he's off and away. As I make to run after him then the coppers grab me by the arms and bundle me into the office.

"Tomas!"

They force me into the one chair in the room and the first copper holds me there while the second one runs out after Tomas, locking the door behind him.

And then I lose it.

It takes over an hour for Sand to arrive from Manchester and by then I'm in a bad way. I think Sand was already on his way – following me by car to York once I'd put the phone down on him – and diverted to Leeds once I got off the train. It still takes him over an hour, though. I haven't seen Tomas and all they'll tell me is that he's safe. The suggestion is that he's safe from me. They haven't touched me since I stopped struggling; there wasn't much point after a while in that small room with the door locked. At first they both had to restrain me but since then only the first copper has stayed.

"What's the story then?" he asks after a while.

I don't answer him. I can't think straight.

"You must have done something for them to follow you all this way," he says.

"I haven't done anything," I say.

"Then what?" he asks.

"Then nothing – it's exactly as I told you."

When Sand arrives then I have to be restrained again.

"Where's Tomas, you fat fuck?" I scream.

Sand is composed but then I am being held down.

"He's safe," he says. "We have someone looking after him."

He leans in towards my face and I lash out with my feet, catching him on the shins. As he steps back I bring up my foot and kick at the gut straining over his trousers. The copper holding me down is helped by PC Byrne, who comes into the room from behind Sand. In the confines of the room they can easily pin me down, both my arms and my legs.

"Calm down, you idiot," says Sand. He brushes down the shoe print on his white shirt.

"You fucking moron!" I scream. "You fucking moron!"

"Calm down," he says again. "This won't get us anywhere."

PC Byrne is close to my face and we look at each other. I think if it was anyone else I would spit at her but I don't. She's looking to see if she can release her grip without me going crazy. There's only going to be one loser here, she's saying. I can feel her body pressed hard against my own. The other copper, the Leeds copper, is taking his lead from her. Eventually she relaxes and stands up. Sand stands as far back in the room as the space allows and shakes his head.

"Why did you get off the train?" he asks.

"Because I saw Caitlin, you fucking moron; you dumb fucking thick fucking plodding fucking moron."

"Where did you see her?" he asks.

"On the platform, you thick – "

"Mr Isaacs!" It's PC Byrne. "Just answer the Detective's questions," she says.

"You saw her on the platform on this station? Which platform?"

"The platform I pointed out at the time," I say. "We could see her, she was there."

Sand looks at the Leeds copper behind me.

"Which platform?" he asks again. "What number?"

"How the fuck should I know what number platform? The one that the trains to Manchester come in on, I guess."

"PC Byrne," he says and she leaves the room.

"But she might have got on the train," I say. "Can you check the trains arriving at Piccadilly?"

Sand looks at me sceptically.

"What?" I ask.

"What have you done?" he asks back.

"Oh Christ," I say. "Just fucking check, will you?"

"What did you mean when you said you thought you

might have done something?"

"When?"

"When you called from the station – you said 'I'm scared I may have done something'."

"I don't know," I say. "I was confused. I didn't know what I was saying."

"And where were you going to go? Before you decided to get off the train, that is?"

"I told you, to my mother's."

"Why?"

"Because Tomas would be happy there and I could get my head together."

"Did you call her to tell her you were going?"

"Yes."

"And what did she think?"

"She was pleased; she's always pleased to see her grandson."

"What about her son?"

"What do you mean?"

"Was she pleased to be seeing you? What will she think now if you don't turn up?"

"I'm going to ring her, if I ever get out of here."

PC Byrne comes back in the room and shakes her head.

"You're a long way from ever getting out of here, my friend," says Sand. "Not unless you start making some sense with your answers."

"If she's not on the platform then she got on the train," I say. "Ask Tomas – he saw her."

"We might just do that," says Sand.

"Where is he?" I ask. "With some fucking social worker?"

"He's safe," says Sand again.

"Safe – you mean safe from me, don't you?"

"Well you have to admit you've been acting pretty strange?"

"Who wouldn't? Tell me – what's normal here?"

"Why did you run away from the school this morning?"

I look at PC Byrne.

"Because I thought I saw Tomas's father."

"But you didn't?"

"Not if PC Byrne says she was speaking to him at the same time. I must have been mistaken."

"But you still ran?"

"I panicked."

"Like when you decided to get off the train? You realised we'd be waiting for you in York and you panicked."

"I saw Caitlin," I say.

"Why would she be in Leeds station?" he asks.

"Because…because, I don't know. I just know I saw her and I know that Tomas saw her." I turn to PC Byrne. "Please just check with Tomas – ask him to show you where he saw her."

She looks to Detective Sand and he nods his approval.

"Actually, sir," says the Leeds copper, "we do have a crazy – a woman – on one of the platforms asking for the train to Manchester. We tell her she's on the wrong platform but she keeps asking anyway."

"You go along with PC Byrne," Sand says to the Leeds copper.

"Will you be alright here, sir?"

"Yes," says Sand, "leave us alone," and then he closes and locks the door.

I realise I'm crying; that tears are falling down my face. Sand lets me be for a few minutes.

"What the fuck is wrong with you?" he asks.

I look at him. He's standing above me and I could easily kick out at him again.

"You mean why am I crying?"

"No, I mean what's wrong with you? What's your problem with the world?"

I don't reply but I do know what he means.

"It's not just the police, is it? It's everyone – social workers, teachers – anyone who's just trying to do their job; everyone you come across then you seem to have some issue with. Why can't you just get along?"

I shrug my shoulders.

"Mr Isaacs?"

"What – yes, I mean?"

"Why did you get off the train?"

"Because I saw Caitlin," I say.

"But why would she be in Leeds station?" he asks again.

I take my time and I try to reply.

"Because just before Tomas was born Caitlin ran away from her husband. He was beating her up and she'd tried to leave but couldn't. When she went back then he beat her up again and this time she thought he was going to kill their baby. She'd already lost one baby and I'm not sure if that wasn't his fault – I don't know about that. So the next day she left him again. She was living in Leeds at the time and she came here, to this station. She came here when she finally managed to get away."

Sand nods and waits for me to continue.

"When...when we were told that we couldn't have children then Caitlin just freaked. I didn't know what to do – either for myself or for Caitlin – and I still don't know. I think she thought...no, I don't know what she thought. She was scared I was going to leave her."

Sand smiles.

"Somebody has to like you, I guess," he says.

"Very funny." I continue. "The couple in the flat upstairs are often fighting – as in, he hits her and we can hear it. They had a bad fight last Sunday night and it was the last thing Caitlin needed to hear. And then when she went back to work the next day she was given the case of that Irish family and, whatever else may have happened afterwards, for Caitlin there would just have been these children without a home."

I look up at Sand.

"I told you that yesterday," I say and again he nods in agreement. "So when Caitlin didn't come home on Monday night, I didn't think 'Oh, she must be in Leeds station going out of her mind'; but when I saw her then it figured because this was the lowest point in her life and I think she believes she's back here, or there."

There's a knock at the door and Sand reaches over to let in PC Byrne.

"Yes," she says, "Tomas was able to show us to his mother."

"And is he with her now?" I ask.

"Yes, but she doesn't know him. I think she's very sick. I've called for a doctor and I thought it best to leave her where she is for now."

"Can I go to her?" I ask PC Byrne and then I look at Sand.

"Yes," he says, "you're free to go."

I stand up in the small room and the three of us are pushed close together – Sand's big fat gut, PC Byrne's sexuality and my resentment.

"Mr Isaacs," says Sand as I walk through the door. "We can arrange a car for you, once we confirm that Ms O'Connor will be OK."

I look at him and know that he's still not sure about me – I might after all have something to do with Caitlin's disappearance.

"No thanks," I say. "We'll wait for the next train."

I walk across the station concourse and up the steps of the bridge to get to Caitlin's platform. This must have once been the platform for the Manchester train. I can see from the top of the steps that Tomas is holding Caitlin's hand but that she's continuing her own private conversation as though he weren't there. The Leeds copper is standing to one side.

"Tomas," I call and when he sees me he lets go of Caitlin's hand and comes running over. I kneel down to greet him and we hug.

"It's like she doesn't know me," he says.

"Give her a moment or two," I say.

"Will she be OK?" he asks.

"Let's go and ask her."

He hesitates and looks from me to Caitlin. She's back to looking along the tracks for the next train. I can see how sick Caitlin is, weak and dehydrated but most of all confused.

"Go on," I say, "but slowly."

I walk with Tomas, my hand on his shoulder.

"Mum," he says and she turns around. She looks at Tomas and doesn't react and I'm scared that she's about to turn away again. Tomas looks up at me and then tries again.

"Mum?"

He takes a step forward and reaches for Caitlin's hand. At his touch, she looks down and then looks towards me.

"Tomas," she says.

"That's right," I say. "It's Tomas, your son. Our son."

I can see the struggle of confusion in her eyes but I can also see that the tiredness is going to win; hopefully, finally she can give in. She looks around helplessly.

"My suitcase," she says.

"Your suitcase is at home," I say.

"At home?" More confusion.

"In Manchester," I say.

"I was on a train…"

"So were we," says Tomas encouraged. "We were going to Grandma Annie's but then we found you."

He looks at me to see where this leaves the whole Grandma Annie trip. I smile at him. He looks back at Caitlin. Grandma Annie will understand.

Towards spring – sometime in early March – we're out walking in the park. The puppies are old enough to be out and Tomas is keen to try out his new bike. We're scared that when we let the puppies loose they might never come back but the opposite happens – they cling to us like they're still on their leads, looking up at Caitlin and myself for instructions on what to do.

"Call them," I shout to Tomas and, as he steadies himself with the bike, they hear him and are torn. As Tomas sets off once more on his bike, their instinct to round him up kicks in and they're away.

We paid the full price for Tomas's bike in a shop. Suzie said she could have found us one for next to nothing but by then it was bought and paid for. Once Caitlin was out of hospital Suzie acted as though nothing had happened over those few days in January and I think her attitude is for the best – why go back over things? Olivia just smiles and makes me feel good about myself. We put PC Byrne on to John upstairs and he's been missing now for over a month: what's the point in staying if you're not free to kick the shit out your wife? Of course, we didn't tell Sarah what we'd done and I can sympathise – she doesn't know where John might be. Imran left our lives as quickly as he'd arrived but it's freaky to know he's out there.

I'm about to become Tomas's legal guardian so hopefully we won't be hearing from Social Services again. Caitlin has a form of dementia but spends most of her time with us these days – not in the past. We know that long term we have to move away from here, start a new life some place else. I may even have to find a job.

The puppies aren't a solution but they're a start.

A teenager on a motorbike, a scrambling bike, roars into

the park and then races along the footpath, doing a wheelie.

"What a prick!" I say quietly to Caitlin.

He cuts away from the path, across the grass to where the puppies are chasing Tomas. The puppies start yelping at the noise and commotion. Tomas looks behind him to see what's happening and wavers unsteadily on his pushbike. The motorbike's so close to Tomas that I know it has to hit him. It happens so quickly – Caitlin grasps my arm and I see for myself how it must have been when my father was killed.

The motorbike speeds away and we run to Tomas but he's OK, shaken and confused by the noise but otherwise unhurt. We can see where the motorbike has cut up tracks in the wet grass, deliberately missing Tomas by only inches.

As I put the puppies back on their leads, the motorbike comes back for a second run. We stand there together – a family of five – Caitlin's arm on Tomas' shoulder, her other hand holding my sleeve while I try to steady the dogs. We watch silently as the bike speeds past. The teenager skids the motorbike around and brakes to a stop a short distance away. Leaving his engine running, he takes off his helmet and looks at us, specifically at me.

"What?" he asks. "What's your problem?"

I shake my head.

"Nothing," I say. "Nothing at all."